Jimmy McCarthy's Truck

Kevin Bjork

Jimmy McCarthy's Truck

by Kevin Bjork
Copyright © 2020, 2022, Kevin Bjork.
Published by Marea Anderson Designs
PO Box 25443, St. Paul, MN 55125

Editor: Marea Anderson
Production Editor: Marea Anderson
Copy editors: Marea Anderson, Elizabeth Willard
Proofreader: Dave Polacek
Cover Designer: Marea Anderson
Interior Designer: Marea Anderson
Illustrator: Marea Anderson

ISBN 978-1-387-58452-9

To Ev and the boys

For the staff and residents at Greeley,
Good Sam, and Linden

I look back now with an innocent tear

Growing old becomes a desperate fear

Still feel the wind in my hair

I daydream that I'm still there

Just runnin' around in Jimmy McCarthy's

truck

Molly Scheer

From *Jimmy McCarthy's Truck*

Introduction

Kevin Bjork's funny, beautiful and moving story follows Frank McCarthy, a resident at Willow Manor nursing home. When we meet Frank he is surrounded by a collection of wonderfully odd people with a variety of eccentricities and needs of care; in other words, absolutely normal human beings. He gives us just enough detail to render a true feeling for the place, searching out common ground between the seemingly disparate characters. The narrative is not sugar-coated. Life and death are real players in this game.

Most special in Frank's life is Alice. They complement each other in words and abilities. The comfort of their patter tells us their relationship has long passed the fear of embarrassment or hurt feelings. Their conversations are true gems. Bjork has a keen ear for dialogue, using it both to reveal their growing love for each other and to consistently move the plot forward.

The other prominent figure in Frank's life is Jimmy, his grandson. Jimmy is on his own journey, trying to keep the family farm afloat and finding time to wet a fishing line. This leaves him perilously unprepared and unaware of any upcoming romance, which opens the door for Frank to set in motion the driving action of the story. If all great stories are love stories this certainly puts *Jimmy McCarthy's Truck* in the pantheon.

Bjork has a way of baiting a memory like a fish, coaxing it to the surface and bringing it home. He masterfully finds the divine in the everyday, the beauty of being human and the cost; however hilarious and heartfelt, frail and powerful. His characters remind us to savor the moments, the graceful passing through the thresholds of our lives. We are left remembering when "it doesn't get any better than this".

Like Jimmy's river, sometimes you're in the current, sometimes watching from the shore. There's the surface we see and the hidden underneath, the things we know and the unseen treasures. There is a bounty of treasure in this book.

Kevin Kling, American storyteller, author, playwright, regular commentator on NPR's *All Things Considered*.

Prologue

Paper charts were strewn about the center island of the nursing station on the med-surg unit of our community hospital. Several physicians chatted among themselves on this late summer Saturday morning in 1994, while rummaging within those charts for notes from previous admissions and emergency room visits, past medical history and current medications, lab and x-ray reports; then scribbling their own progress notes and new orders. In a few years this process would be forever transformed by an electronic medical record.

A nurse came out of room 124 to inform me that Mrs. O'Brien had swallowed her gallstones. Looking up, I asked "she what?"

"Alice wanted to take them home to show her granddaughter. The lab sent them over in a specimen cup and I put it on her tray table. She thought they were just more pills so she screwed off the lid and swallowed 'em with a sip of water; said they were crunchy and a little salty, but not bad. By the way, she's anxious to get out of here, says she has a lot to do at home."

"I'm surprised she was able to open it with her arthritis. Does she know that her daughters have her set up to go back to the nursing home?"

"She does and isn't very happy about it. Alice has had an interesting life, but she's been pretty depressed the past few years and it sounds like things weren't going well when she was at home."

"I just met her for the first time last weekend. I'll have more time to talk with her when we go over her discharge plans."

Alice had been brought to the hospital from a local nursing home by ambulance, with severe abdominal pain. She had arrived the previous Sunday when the CT-on-a-truck wasn't available, and an ultrasound had shown stones in her gallbladder and lab work confirmed inflammation of her pancreas, likely caused by passage of a gallstone. She had been critically ill on admission, but her pain and labs improved over the next few days and her gallbladder had been removed laparoscopically, with an uneventful recovery after surgery. Social services had spent time with Alice and her daughters going over her discharge planning which included a higher level of care at Willow Manor.

After exiting Alice's room a half hour later I re-engaged her chart and mentioned a bit about her childhood to a senior family doc, also at the table, who was writing orders for a patient admitted during the night with congestive heart failure.

She put down her pen and suggested that I write down the stories of some of these patients, "something to look back on. We are fortunate to cross paths with a lot of seemingly random people in our community; the same folks we walk by on the street or stand next to in a check-out line, but we have the privilege of a more intimate relationship with them. For you that may be a relatively brief encounter lasting a few days, like taking out a gallbladder and moving on. For me, it may be a lifetime of care, from bringing them into this world to end-of-life issues and everything in between."

After her discharge I saw Alice a few more times at the nursing home when I was there seeing other patients. I wrote down some of what she told me in a notebook that, along with the stories of other patients, became three notebooks which I stacked on a shelf with a couple other notebooks of personal recollections and ruminations. The following pages are my attempt to use a contrived storyline to meld those notebooks together.

Chapter One

Rudy Vandevusse was a farmer from across the river who had been diagnosed two years earlier with Lou Gehrig's disease. By the time of diagnosis he was already disabled from the neuromuscular wasting that had robbed his strength and made a challenge out of previously taken-for-granted functions like speaking and swallowing. That spring he had legally passed on the farm to his only son.

The farm itself consisted of one hundred and eighty tillable acres growing corn and soybeans, another forty acres of pasture for the sixty Holstein they milked, and some set aside for which they received an annual stipend from the government to leave alone. Like most family farms, they flirted with insolvency every fall. The simple math of bushels harvested times price-per-bushel, minus bank notes due, determined whether, come the following spring, they would still be on the farm that had been in the family for over eighty years.

Rudy's rapidly declining health was less of a concern to him than getting his son off to a good start. He was pleased when a warm, dry spring allowed planting ahead of schedule and was joyous when the soaking rains came two days after the seed was in the ground. It was during this hectic time of planting, calving, and milking he realized the burden he had become to his family and, against their wishes, decided to be admitted to Willow Manor.

He told them it would be temporary, just until things slowed down on the farm but knew, as he was being lifted into the wheelchair-adapted van, that this chapter of his life was over. He hoped to be back a few times to visit and was buoyed at the sight of vigorous ankle-high sprouts as the van coursed the dusty gravel leading away from the only home he had ever known.

Five weeks later Rudy slept in as the nighttime rain, which had ended a nearly three week drought, continued to fall on the cars outside his window at Willow Manor. The other residents had awoken to begin another day in a world that, in their youth, had seemed so remote and bizarre, but was now their reality.

Tillie Millborne ate breakfast with both the first and second sittings. Paralyzed from the waist down and bursting out of her wheelchair, from too many calories and too little exercise, Tillie was allowed two full breakfasts. This was partly because of her love for eating, but mostly because of her love for talking. She had a captive audience at both sittings and extolled her opinions of the topics covered the evening before on ABC news by the love of her life, Peter Jennings. A former librarian, Tillie was legally blind, but her thick glasses and large-print books allowed her to continue her other passion - reading. However, as it became more difficult to process the written word, she became increasingly reliant on being spoon-fed verbally by network television.

Frank McCarthy and Alice O'Brien ate breakfast together and spent most of the morning playing cribbage in Frank's room. Frank managed the cards and moved the pegs for both of them with his left hand; his right hand paralyzed from the stroke that had brought him to Willow Manor. Alice was unable to manage her own cards and pegs due to hands crippled by the arthritis that had brought her there. Jack was the RN who had admitted Frank when he first arrived at Willow Manor. He was working on another wing of the nursing home that rainy morning but stopped by to see how the card game was going.

"Quite a storm last night. Did it keep you two awake?"

Frank responded that there had been "a nice bolt of lightning just outside the window with thunder that really shook the place, otherwise slept through most of it."

"I've got a pretty awful lightning story for you two if you want to hear it" Jack offered.

"Sure," Alice chimed in, "we've got time... lots of it".

"I was at the '91 US Open Golf Tourney at Hazeltine over in Chaska. Payne Stewart won it, but I was following Lee Trevino. He and Corey Pavin were coming down the sixteenth fairway. The stands around the green were full so I just stood off to the side. Pavin is lining up his shot, maybe a hundred fifty yards out, when there's lightning in the distance and the horn goes off. Trevino was gone before I even turned around 'cause I think he had issues with lightning in the past.'

"So it starts raining really hard and I get some shelter under this willow tree with four other guys I don't know. There were bigger trees around, but they were already crowded with folks trying to stay dry. There's an announcement that it will be at least a half hour before they can resume, so we decided to get some beers. I offered to go get them, and scooted through the rain to the concession stand about thirty yards away. I'm under the awning paying for the beers and a bratwurst when there was this amazing flash of light and a crack followed by screams and commotion coming from where I had just been.'

"I ran over there and the four guys I had been with were laid out like bowling pins; shoes blown off their feet, hair singed off their heads, not moving, smell of burnt flesh in the air. I started working on one guy who I think survived. It took a long time for the ambulance to get there. At least one of the guys died under that tree and another may have died later at the hospital. Really freaked me out. Since then, anytime somebody needs to go fetch something, I'm all over it."

"Quite a story Jack, can you fetch me a beer? I get one a day"

"I know you do, Leinenkugel. I can see that you're really impressed by my story. You'll have to ask your real nurse. Take care you two. Alice, you need to watch Frank with the cards. His sleight of hand is well known around this place."

The rain would continue throughout an otherwise quiet day at Willow Manor - no ambulance runs to the local hospital, no outbursts, no deaths.

———————

Joe Jankey had been in the first group to eat breakfast. His face had been wiped clean, his bib taken off and he was now on his way to physical therapy for rehab after a left below-knee amputation for a gangrenous foot three weeks earlier. He had had two previous vascular bypasses to prolong the inevitable, but genetics and diabetes finally took their toll.

Nobody knew where to find walleyes on the St. Croix like Joe, or "Shoes" as he was nicknamed in high school for his size thirteen feet. When he had come back from surgery Jack was his nurse. An avid baseball fan whose favorite movie was *Field of Dreams*, Jack had helped him to bed and wondered whether to make light of the situation by calling him "Shoe" and at some point "Shoeless Joe" since his remaining foot didn't look much better than the one that had been amputated.

For his part Joe seemed totally oblivious to the lost limb, being far more interested in talking about spring walleyes just offshore north of Wolf Marina. Jack wrote this off to either confusion from medications or early dementia, but when Joe began talking about "Stumpy" Jack realized that he knew exactly what had been done and he saw a toughness and resilience in Joe's eyes that had previously escaped him. He thought of what Joe's generation had gone through and how it had prepared them for the trials of elder age.

———————

The previous evening Rudy had been out on the patio with Frank and Alice. He wondered and worried to himself when the nearly three-week drought would end. Rudy's son had told him that the corn was holding up fine, but he could visualize the wilting and browning of his son's deed to the property and dreamt at night of blistered stalks scattered across a parched earth with cracks into which he would find himself falling. He had been oblivious to the musings of the pair regarding the destination of a passing train as he scanned the horizon for any cloud formation that foretold the possibility of rain.

Rudy's well-being worsened with a pneumonia he didn't have the strength to clear. IV antibiotics and incentive coughing and breathing had kept the infection in check. Later that night he was awoken at four o'clock in the morning to the sound of thunder, which confused him at first because the evening sky had been clear, and the forecast had called for increasing humidity with just a thirty-percent chance of showers.

Unable to lift himself, he pushed the nurse light and, a few minutes later, was leaning forward in his wheelchair peering out the window as the first big drops of rain plopped against the glass. Rudy strained to lift his right arm to open the window so he could feel the life-giving, farm-saving rain. Halfway up it went limp and fell back in his lap. Leaning further forward and giving the right arm a boost with his left he got the arm up onto the windowsill and slid it forward to where he could clumsily flip the latch with his knuckles and push the window open. A cold, wet gust of air caught him square in the face with a freshness that filled his senses as he leaned his head back with closed eyes and sucked it in.

He barely moved for the next hour and half as the thunder rolled, and the rain poured, except to turn and growl at the nurses who tried to close the window. As the raucous storm settled into a nearly silent, windless drizzle Rudy fell asleep with the left side of his face smashed against the windowsill. A nurse quietly closed the window and gently put a pillow under his head.

Rudy missed breakfast, but awoke for lunch, eating half of the turkey and all the mashed potatoes, gravy, creamed corn, and apple crumble. Back in his room he watched the rain out of the window most of the afternoon, his deep cough worsening with periodic shaking chills. He appeared feverish, but wouldn't allow his temperature to be taken.

In the late afternoon Rudy's son arrived with a videotape. David frequently brought movies that they would watch together, never saying much, but it was cherished time together for both. Rudy wasn't much in the mood for a movie, but didn't complain as David popped the tape in the VCR. A quick rewind and half-a-minute of Taylor's third birthday party gave way to a wide-angle view of the farm with puddles in the yard and driveway as the rain fell. The screen was soon filled with rows of thigh-high corn gently blowing in the wet breeze.

For several minutes Rudy watched rain falling on the corn with a charge that had begun with the early morning thunderclap. When the screen went to gray static Rudy motioned for the remote. David put it under his hand on the wheelchair arm and Rudy hit the rewind until it was again back at the birthday party, which was followed again by the rain on the farm, rain on the corn. David saw the mist in his dad's eyes.

"A real soaker, Dad. Watch close and you can actually see the corn growing."

Rudy nodded, eyes on the screen and then looked back at David. There was a lot he wanted to say, but his mouth would no longer form the words as the mist turned to droplets, which slid haltingly down his cheeks.

"Dad, we're going to be okay. Thanks for your help." There was more that David wanted to say but the exact words escaped him. "Well, I'd better head back home. Take care of yourself. That cough doesn't sound good. I'll stop back tomorrow with Taylor."

Jack was charge nurse that night and started his shift at 10:30. The evening nurse had reported that Rudy wasn't doing well and when Jack checked on him Rudy was still watching the tape for the umpteenth time, his cough and chills getting worse. He snapped at Jack's suggestion to go back to bed and purposely emptied his bladder into his wheelchair after Jack had left, temporarily enjoying the warmth it brought to his groin and thighs.

"What the hell?" he thought, "in a few hours I'll be dead anyway and they'll just think I did it when I died. I'll probably lose my bowels too, with some vomit drooling out of my mouth." He smiled to himself at this last act of recklessness.

Urine was the only cleanup necessary when Rudy's nurse found him slumped forward in his wheelchair at 2:00 a.m. with only the safety strap keeping him from falling out. Rosa checked his pulse, found none, and reaffirmed from Rudy's chart that he was "*do not resuscitate.*" She called Jack after turning off the tape, which Rudy had rewound to the beginning and was now showing a farmhouse Christmas with a jolly Santa who looked like a younger Rudy handing out gifts to an excited pack of kids.

Jack had been an RN at Willow Manor for six years, gradually taking on more administrative responsibilities but still working as a floor nurse most of the time. He had met Frank's grandson, Jimmy McCarthy, shortly after Frank's arrival at Willow Manor. They had gotten to talking about fishing and Jack had mentioned that he often fly-fished for trout on the Rush River upstream from Martel. Jimmy knew exactly where he was referring because the family of a high school friend farmed the land adjacent to the section of stream Jack wanted to fish. He had hunted and fished there himself.

Jimmy described the farm and Jack remembered having asked for permission to access the river through that property; but had been denied because of previous damage to fences, littering and pasture gates being left open by other fishermen. Unable to access that stretch of stream Jack had usually just fished closer to town.

Although Jimmy preferred fishing for pike he and Jack made plans to spend a morning chasing trout. Jack said it was OK for Jimmy to bring along one of his buddies.

Chapter Two

The annual running of the bulls at the San Fermin Festival in Pamplona had gone fifteen years without a death prior to the goring of Matthew Tassio. The magazine photo had shown the right-curved horn of the massive roan piercing the right chest of the 22-year-old college student from Illinois on that narrow cobblestone street. It was a vivid image in the old man's mind as he sat on a kelly-green canvas lawn chair with an aluminum frame in the middle of the street, near the end of the nine-hundred-yard course the bulls thundered along en route to the coliseum.

The street ahead of him had mostly cleared as the daredevil crowd running with the bulls had thinned, allowing him to stare directly at the dozen or so charging animals, now fewer than fifty yards away. A khaki-clad officer wearing designer sunglasses and toting a short-handled, sawed-off shotgun emerged from the crowd and strode briskly toward the old man.

Looking directly at the officer, the old man calmly reached his right hand into a brown leather satchel on the ground by his side. Above the roar of the crowd and the stampeding bulls the officer heard a distinctive metal click and backed off. With the bulls now within thirty yards, the old man pulled his hand out of the satchel and clicked the top on a can of Leinenkugel's twice more to settle the foam before opening it. He savored the first unhurried swallow of beer as it washed the dust from his mouth and throat and cleared his sinuses.

He lowered the can from his face, allowing himself to better see the wild-eyed, well-horned beasts with broad, heaving chests, spraying dust and mucous tinged with blood from their flared nostrils. He wondered if the front bulls would go around him or trample him directly.

The rumbling ground awakened Frank as a Burlington Northern freight train passed sixty yards from the north side of the nursing home where he had stayed the past eight months while recovering from a stroke. He still needed a wheelchair to get around because of right-sided weakness and rigidity, but the left facial paralysis, his inability to speak, and his difficulty in swallowing had mostly resolved. Facing west and enjoying the midsummer twilight in his wheelchair on the front porch, he had dozed off. The sun was now down, but its presence was still apparent through orange rays illuminating a few scattered cumulus clouds near the horizon.

"Where do you suppose she'll be come morning?" he inquired of the 38-year-old male nurse who had also stepped out to take in the end of the day.

"I imagine she'll stop over at the Northtown yard in Fridley, change a few cars, and head west sometime after midnight. Suppose she'll be up around Fargo-Moorhead when the sun comes up."

"Sounds like you know a bit about freight trains, Jack."

"After Arlo Guthrie told me about his father's magic carpet made of steel and reading *Rolling Nowhere* by Ted Conover I got the bug. Took a couple free trips west, courtesy of Burlington Northern and Santa Fe. Even had a friend who worked at BN get me computerized schedules, so I knew which trains were going where and when they were going to leave.

"How about you, Frank, ever ride the rails?" Jack asked.

"Actually did for a while back in the Depression. My best friend and I both lost our jobs about the same time. We couldn't find anything in Milwaukee where we lived and couldn't afford a car or bus fare, so we hopped trains from town to town, along with a lot of other guys. You've probably seen the pictures of a couple dozen fellas hanging off a train. Well, that was us. We took whatever work we could find: odd jobs, farm work, factory labor. If we couldn't both stay working, we moved on. The summer evenings on the train, just before dark, were the best. We saw more incredible sunsets from the doorway of a boxcar, always wondering where we'd be come morning."

"Where's your buddy now?"

"He died a few years later at Normandy."

"Normandy? I just read the Newsweek article on the fiftieth anniversary of Normandy. Were you there too?"

"Yeah, I'd probably be over there for the reunion right now if it wasn't for the stroke."

"What beach did you go in on?"

"Omaha."

The Newsweek story raced through Jack's mind, from the gourmet breakfast on ship at four o'clock that morning, through the slaughter on the beach, the accounts of incredible courage and the significance of the landing. The only response that came to Jack was "thanks for what you guys did."

Jack waited for Frank to say more. When he didn't, Jack stepped around behind Frank's wheelchair, unlocked the brakes, commented on the mosquitoes which were just coming out and wheeled Frank past the gray brick fountain in the narrow courtyard, through the nursing home entrance and into the lobby where the Thursday night bingo game was in full swing. Half the residents managed their own cards. Several had their cards managed by staff or family, and the rest were just parked in wheelchairs with unmarked bingo cards on their laps and no expressions on their faces.

"Want to watch the tarpon video?" Frank asked Jack as Elsie Holmberg was wheeled up to the front to have her card checked to see if she indeed had a four-corner bingo.

Jack looked at his watch, "Sure, I can punch out early. Let me go give report and I'll be right down."

Jack had met Frank in the same way he had met most of his stroke patients. Frank had been transferred to Willow Manor after five days in the hospital, two of which were spent on the respirator. He had come by non-emergent ambulance and was wheeled into his room on a cart.

The paramedic had given Jack a brief review of his hospital stay and told him Frank had been stable during the transfer. Frank had stared straight ahead through glazed eyes and drooled from the paralyzed left corner of his mouth. Since he had been unable to swallow, a feeding tube had been placed through his nose into his stomach. They would be using that to give him nutrition, fluids and medications while waiting to see if his ability to swallow would return. If it didn't, he would either need to have a more permanent tube placed endoscopically through his upper left abdominal wall and into his stomach, or he would be allowed to die of starvation. He also had a bladder catheter and got oxygen through a nasal canula.

After helping transfer Frank's rigid body into bed, Jack went over his admitting orders with the charge nurse, which included his tube feeding formula, multiple medications, speech and physical therapy, activity and restraint orders, pressure sore precautions, and a do-not-resuscitate status in the event of cardiac or respiratory arrest. Jack had told the charge nurse that if he ever showed up at Willow Manor in that kind of shape, he'd only need one order: a hundred milligrams of morphine as an IV push.

Over the next week, however, Frank began showing signs of being more aware of his environment, and more understanding of what was being told to him. His swallowing also improved over the next two weeks to where his diet was slowly advanced, and the feeding tube removed. His grandson, Jimmy, brought in a bunch of pictures - an old wedding photo of Frank and his wife Betty, another picture of Betty in her apron on the farmhouse porch, one of Jimmy and his sister who now lived in California, a couple pictures of Frank's farm across the river in Wisconsin, a picture of Frank and Jimmy getting off a chair lift, and another picture of Frank and Jimmy with the faces of four presidents carved into the side of a mountain in the background. Jimmy had mounted the pictures on a small bulletin board and tacked the board to the plaster wall adjacent to Frank's bed.

Late one night while cleaning Frank up after an involuntary bowel movement, Jack noticed the pictures on the wall and spent a few moments glancing back and forth from the pictures of Frank's younger days to his current pitiful state. Jack didn't think much more of it, until Jimmy stopped by a couple of days later. Jimmy had told Jack how Frank had grown up on a farm in Oklahoma, but had moved north when the well had gone dry during the dust bowl. Frank's father had died of pneumonia leaving Frank, the oldest, to support their family of seven in Milwaukee. The work was scarce, so he had traveled from job to job and sent the money back home. His last job had been as a hired hand on the farm he and Frank currently lived on.

The owner had two sons die in World War II and had left Frank the farm when he died, although it was still heavily mortgaged. Frank had outlived his own wife and two children.

Over the next month Frank's condition improved significantly with speech that progressed from guttural grunts and groans, to garbled - but understandable - words and phrases. Physical therapy worked with him twice a day and the passive and active range-of-motion and strengthening exercises began showing results. The pictures and talk with Jimmy had put Frank into a bit of a different light for Jack than the other stroke patients, most of whom were not showing the progress Frank was.

Jack made an extra effort to make sure Frank was comfortable and worked with him on his speech and mobility between therapy sessions. Frank took a liking to Jack and his face would light up when Jack popped into his room. He seemed quieter and more withdrawn on Jack's days off.

As he entered Frank's room, Jack closed the door behind him and turned on the fan pointed toward the open window. He handed Frank a cold beer and Frank pulled a Dominican cigar out of his dresser drawer and gave it to Jack. He himself had quit smoking cigarettes twenty years prior, but had still enjoyed an occasional cigar, until the stroke. Frank was allowed a beer a day, per doctor's orders, which he had already been given that afternoon, but Jack gave him another without charting it.

Frank's beer open and Jack's cigar lit, Jack popped in the promo tape from the Silver King Lodge in Costa Rica, which Frank had picked up at the Minneapolis Sportsmen's Show two years prior. His grandson, Jimmy, loved fishing and Frank had hoped to someday take him on a fishing trip he would never forget. Maybe Jack would come too.

Even though they had watched the tape several times before, each jump the tackle-busting tarpon made brought animated reactions from both. They decided that the perfect day would start with a big breakfast at the lodge, washed down with strong Costa Rican coffee. Morning would be spent in outboards offshore casting for the big boys. Lunch back at the lodge would be followed by a couple hours' siesta in the hammocks on the porch. Late afternoon would find them heading up the Rio Colorado in search of the smaller, but even stronger river tarpon. Cocktails back at the lodge would precede surfcasting for snook at sunset, to be then cooked over an open fire on the beach as tales of fish caught and missed were relived. As the fire reduced to embers, a full moon rising over the turquoise gulf waters would give them enough light to find their way back to the lodge as their perfect day came to a close.

The tape was finished, the empty beer can and cigar butt were placed in a red plastic bag. The top was tied, and the bag dropped out of the open window. They knew their method of getting rid of the contraband was overdone, but it added to the moment. Pine-scented Lysol was generously sprayed around the room.

"You working tomorrow?"

"Yeah, I'll be here."

A minute later, a shadowy figure approached a now-closed window, stooped over and then crossed the parking lot. Frank watched the silhouette as the dumpster was opened, the bag dropped in, and the lid closed. He watched as his friend started his car, backed up and drove off. He stared out the window a few more minutes, thinking it had been a pretty good night, good enough that he had forgotten for a while why he was there. A twinge of pain in his left hip brought him back and he pushed the nurse light. A couple of pain pills allowed him to get to sleep before his roommate had even gotten back from bingo.

Tony Mihalik had grown up playing hockey in northern Minnesota. He had made it as far as the farm team for Montreal. His progressive dementia had made caring for him at home too difficult for his wife. His snoring made sleeping in the same room difficult for Frank.

Having watched the previous Super Bowl, Frank knew that many of the marquee players had worn Breathe-Rite nasal strips. He also had read that by pulling out the soft cartilage on the sides of the nose, thereby widening the airway, some benefit was possible for snorers, so he had Jack buy a box. That first night, shortly after Tony had drifted into his room-rattling snore, Jack helped him over to Tony's bed. With Frank's right hand nearly useless, Jack had assisted him in gently placing a strip across the bridge of Tony's oft-broken, now-angled nose, exactly how Jerry Rice had worn his. Tony snuffed and snorted. He brushed his forearm against his nose as if brushing away a fly, but he never woke up, and the strip stayed in place.

Frank had his best night's sleep in several weeks, with the only sounds being the usual ones: cleaning carts and nurses passing in the hallway, a thud followed by a groan followed by a half hour of commotion as Hap Hanson fell out of bed, broke his hip and was taken by ambulance to the hospital. At 3:30, there was Ruth Gunderson singing "Amazing Grace," which trailed off into a muffled sob near the end of the second stanza, and at 5:30, Katie Coughlan could be heard banging on the emergency exit from her wheelchair, "Open the door and let me in, Lord Jesus. I'm ready to come home. I've been a sinner all my life, but I'm ready to come home. Lord Jesus...." Then louder after a pause, "Open the goddamned door!"

But Tony was mostly silent, and Frank slept straight through until 7:00 a.m. He joined Alice for breakfast. She had become absorbed in the OJ trial. Her late husband had been a public defender for Ramsey County. William had believed strongly in the judicial system and in the right of every citizen to proper representation. After law school, he had been offered the job and had accepted it out of a genuine desire to represent the less fortunate of our society. Over the next thirty-four years, William would, on occasion, show disappointment or frustration with a particular case, but never cynicism of the system itself. William was not one to leave his work at the office, so he and Alice frequently discussed the interesting cases he was involved in. Through him Alice had become quite knowledgeable about courtroom strategies and maneuverings.

The OJ trial rekindled in Alice an interest in judicial process that had lain dormant since William's sudden death from a massive heart attack six years earlier. The daily television and print coverage were similar to the daily dialogue she and William had, the obvious difference being that the OJ trial was on a far grander scale in every aspect; with the slow freeway chase of a famous defendant in his white Ford Bronco, big-name defenders, seemingly insurmountable evidence, and a cast of witnesses that Hollywood couldn't duplicate.

Alice took it all in and hung on every word out of Marcia Clark's mouth, from her opening statement to the video montage closing argument. Here was an unheard-of female county prosecutor going toe-to-toe with the big boys of defense law. She sympathized when Marcia's home situation deteriorated as the trial went on. She changed her hairstyle every time Marcia did. She came to detest "the scheme team", as Johnny Cochrane and F. Lee Bailey played the race card and "off the bottom of the deck," as Robert Schapiro would later say. She couldn't believe it when the prosecution allowed OJ to try on the glove that had sat in storage for months which she knew would have shrunk and led to Cochrane's famous *"if the glove doesn't fit, you must acquit."* She became disillusioned with the judicial system in a way her husband never had when a verdict was reached, following very little deliberation, and comments from the jurors indicated that the evidence presented to them had not influenced their decision. The trial had not been a search for truth, which William had felt was the sole purpose of trial law.

After the trial, Alice went through the withdrawal that many avid trial fans went through, but soon got over it and, in the end took solace in the fact that William had not seen the circus his beloved judicial system had been turned into.

It was during these months of courtroom drama that Frank

and Alice had become acquainted. Both were mentally sound, but physically challenged. Alice's rheumatoid arthritis had left her with fingers that now angled forty-five degrees away from her thumb side, which meant she needed assistance with nearly all of her daily activities. William had taken early retirement to be with her and never tired of helping her feed or dress herself.

Despite the arthritis, those were some of the best years of their life together; the fast-paced lifestyle had been put aside, truly savoring the time spent together, each knowing that the time was limited. Alice had always assumed that she would be the first to go, with the rheumatoid arthritis finally finishing the job it had pursued relentlessly for decades.

William had no unhealthy habits, except the occasional long pour of single malt and the pipe, which had to be smoked outside by house rules. He exercised regularly and took just a daily blood pressure pill. His sudden death not only quieted the laughter and music in their home, but left Alice with no reason to go through the painful and tedious routines of daily life.

A series of home care nurses and aides were hired and fired over the next few months by a once-vibrant woman, now bitter and lifeless. Exasperated, her daughters had used the need for more nursing help and physical therapy to get Alice to agree on a temporary stay at Willow Manor. Two further attempts at home were unsuccessful and resulted in a return to Willow Manor where Alice remained withdrawn and detached, until the OJ trial.

Previously considered antisocial by most of the other residents, she searched out anyone following the trial that she could compare daily trial notes with. Most of the nurses were following the trial, but were too busy to spend much time talking about it with her. Many of the residents were eager to talk, but had no idea who OJ was before or during the trial, except Frank. Not that he was an avid trial fan like Alice, but he had watched all of the Fuhrman and Kato testimony and also wondered whether the mountains of evidence would have any bearing on the outcome.

Frank mostly listened while Alice talked, occasionally offering opinions on an aspect of the trial or the newest Marcia look-alike hairdo, both enjoying the porch at sunset. When the evening train came by, they would watch silently, equally impressed with the power and mystique. As the train melted into the distant twilight, they would both sit quietly, wheelchairs side by side for a few more minutes before calling for the aides to push them back in. Frank would always ask the same question, and Alice would tell him that particular train would be in Albuquerque or Sacramento or Seattle come sunrise. It was on those nights that they had often been joined by Rudy Vandevusse.

Chapter Three

Jimmy and Jack finally got their schedules together for trout fishing. They met in Hudson in the Fleet Farm parking lot at 5:00 a.m. Jimmy had gotten up two hours earlier to milk and had put off the remaining chores. Jack had asked if he could bring a friend, so Jimmy wasn't surprised to see two guys get out of the maroon '78 Olds Cutlass with white vinyl top, dents in all four quarter panels, and a spider-web crack on the passenger side windshield. They opened the trunk, pulled out their gear, and tossed it into the bed of Jimmy's unblemished '69 candy-apple red Ford pickup. An eighty-pound female black lab peered at them through the back window.

Jack had the Eddie-Bauer-on-a-budget look with a well-worn fishing vest, pockets bulging. A small nail clipper and tape measure hung off the front, a landing net on his left side. Disheveled light brown hair fell to his shoulders under an old Cubs hat. He wore thin-rimmed tortoise-shell glasses. His slight 5'11" frame met the asphalt with a pair of red high-top Converse tennis shoes that would get him to the stream before he changed into hip waders, which had been tossed into the bed of the pickup. Jack gently placed his encased 6 weight fly rod behind the cab.

After putting his gear into the truck, he introduced "Fly." Jimmy needed no explanation of how Fly got his nickname - he had with a stocky build and nearly square face, thick black curly hair ("the only pubic hair he has" Jack had stated matter-of-factly) and oversized black rectangular glasses with coke-bottle lenses. Jimmy figured Fly probably wasn't a real serious trout fisherman as he helped load up Fly's reclining lawn chair and cooler.

"Don't forget your rod," Jack reminded him as Fly started shutting the trunk.

"Oh, yeah," he said, pulling out a stout pole with a Zebco 202 reel. Jimmy would not have been surprised to see a Snoopy logo on the side. Fly had no other tackle with him other than the tennis-ball-sized bobber, quarter-ounce lead weight, and #2 hook already on the line.

Maggie was a good sport about having to ride in the back as Jack and Fly climbed into the cab, with Jack in the middle. On the way to the stream, Jimmy heard several stories from their college days where the two had lived together off campus with Fly's lanky brother Larva and a kid with a last name of Taggetts (Maggot).

He also heard about a rugby tour to Australia that Jack and Fly had been a part of as equipment managers. The tour entourage of eighty included two men's teams and a women's team, with many of the players on all three teams having been friends of theirs from college. The teams had played well during matches in Sydney, Manley Beach, Newcastle, Brisbane, and Coonabarabran.

Jack and Fly had gone on a side trip to the north coast where they went scuba diving on the Barrier Reef, deep sea fishing, and whitewater rafting. This had been capped off by a relaxing night at Barnacle Bill's in Cairns. The team had toured a winery in the Hunter Valley on their way inland to Coonabarabran, and several players plus Jack and Fly had spent a day on horseback at the Knight Ranch helping drive and dehorn cattle. The end of the day had been highlighted by huge flocks of pink cockatoo-like galahs flying across the rolling hills in front of them to their roosts in the tall hardwoods lining the dry creek beds as the cowboy wannabes rode their stock horses back to the ranch house where cold Victoria Bitters, lean beefsteak on white bread and beans were waiting.

Jimmy heard about the post-game social event at the Newcastle team's clubhouse when shortly after midnight, with the beer and songs flowing, and with the party seeming to just be getting started, the place went quiet but for a single Irish tenor. The Newcastle scrumhalf sang "When the Band Played Waltzing Matilda," a song about the massive casualties among the Australian troops at Gallipoli. The Americans had scanned the Aussie players to see the no-neck props, the strapping forwards, and the athletic backs listening solemnly, misty eyes within bruised faces. After the song's completion, the players had silently set down their remaining beers, bid their new mates a good night and walked out of the clubhouse. Just like that, the bar had closed down and, to the Americans' disappointment, the party was over.

Jimmy also heard about how Slurpee had been flown home early from Brisbane by med-evac with a neck injury from the collapse of a scrum. His sister had called a couple days later from a hospital in Minneapolis to let them know that he had started moving his arms and legs again. On arrival back home about half of the team had gone from the airport to the hospital to see him, which was described as "a real shit show" by Fly. Later that spring Slurpee had shown up at practice, with the help of a nine iron as a cane. He looked good and joined them for beers after practice at the Terminal Bar on Hennepin and Central. When Phlegm, the owner, saw Slurpee come through the door he offered the lads an hour of free beer, which rolled into a celebration of friendships borne of shared experiences, recalling stories that needed no embellishment.

Fly had been out late the night before and nodded off a couple of times on the way to the river. As they pulled into the farmyard Jimmy saw light coming from the milk house and pulled up near it. He and Jack hopped out with the engine quietly running and met his friend's father halfway. Fly stayed in the truck and, with increasing daylight, noticed that Jimmy was a couple inches taller than Jack and had uncapped, dirty blond, straight hair that fell to mid-neck and bangs to both eyebrows. He saw a lean profile with a sinewy strength built more by tossing hay bales than barbells. He would later note that Jimmy had a cautious smile and that his eyes could look either green or blue, depending on the light.

After catching up on the latest news concerning his friend's new baby girl and his job as an electrician in Eau Claire, Jimmy had introduced

Walt to Jack and pointed to Fly. Walt assured Jack he could access the stream through his property whenever he wanted, but should call ahead or stop by the house so they would know who was down there. He also reminded them to close the pasture gates.

The dirt farm road followed the edge of a plowed field waiting to be planted and went through a gate, which Fly opened and closed after Jimmy drove through. They crossed a pasture with a couple dozen black-and-white Holsteins, several bulging with soon-to-be-born calves, with a dozen or so calves that looked to be just hours and days old, clinging close to their mothers. They exited the pasture through another gate at the edge of a hardwood forest that sloped down to the river. With mostly just springtime buds on the oaks, maples, and basswood, they could see portions of the river as they followed the dirt road between the fence line and the wood's edge. A quarter mile later, the road veered down the slope and through the woods to the river. It was muddy and deeply rutted, so Jimmy pulled off onto a grassy spot near the top, much to Fly's chagrin since he knew he'd have to walk the rest of the way.

Maggie waited for the tailgate to be dropped before hopping down. Even a year earlier she would have sprung over the sideboards as soon as the truck stopped, but she was slowing down. Nevertheless, the fresh smells of spring and the crisp air charged her up as she raced around in the woods, nose to the ground, following the scents of everything and nothing at the same time. Jimmy was pleased to see her acting like the puppy he remembered so well, but hadn't seen much of lately, with most of her time spent sleeping on the back step or shuffling between the house and barn. Cool mornings were tough for her and that morning she had been very stiff and appeared to be in some pain as she had gotten up and slowly made it to the barn when he went to milk. She was more limber by the time they left to go fishing, but still needed to be lifted into the cab of the truck. Jimmy watched her frolic a few moments before grabbing his fishing vest and spinning gear.

"You got waders?" Jack asked.

"Nah, these are fine," Jimmy responded motioning to his well-worn Red Wing boots.

They had to help Fly haul his stuff to a clearing by the river, but once there he took over. The lawn chair was positioned near the water facing the rising sun with the cooler next to it. A Cub food bag was emptied of pre-packaged pastries, a Star Tribune newspaper, and a blue plastic carton of night crawlers. Jack handed him his fishing rod before putting on his own waders, and he watched Fly bait the hook.

Regular glasses were exchanged for prescription sunglasses and a Summit pale ale was pulled from the cooler and opened. Fly took a good swallow, tucked the bottle under his left arm while he took a piss, watched the steam it produced on hitting the cool, wet earth, shivered and shook before zipping up. He casted his line into a slow-moving pool near shore, stuck the butt end of the rod into the webbing of the lounge chair to hold it, sat down, opened a pastry and the newspaper, stretched out his legs and started fishing.

Jimmy selected a No. 1 Mepps spinner and started downstream; Jack picked a size-18 hare's ear nymph and headed upstream. They would meet back at the clearing at noon. Fly looked up from the newspaper to assure them that he would hold down the fort while they were gone.

Jimmy found a flat rock just offshore he could hop onto, from where he could cast into a nice hole and a couple deep riffles. He hooked, landed, and released a chunky fourteen-inch rainbow that broke water twice on his third cast. He looked upstream to see how Jack and Fly were doing.

Fly looked to be asleep, and Jack was slowly working around the first bend, mid-stream in knee-high water, making flowing arcs with his fly line and softly dropping the delicate fly onto the moving water. He would let it drift eight or ten seconds, mending the line two or three times as he deftly brought in line with his congenitally underdeveloped left arm to avoid getting too much slack. He would then gently lift the fly out of the water, false cast a couple of times, and softly drop the fly again upstream.

Jimmy had never asked Jack about his arm and Jack hadn't brought it up. From what Jimmy could tell the disability didn't seem to restrict him much. At Willow Manor he was able to do everything the job required despite the flesh-colored foam rubber brace that extended from just above his elbow to the middle of his hand, with just the fingers and knuckles being visible.

Jimmy watched Jack for a few minutes, thinking how the grace of his fly presentation matched the grace of this splendid Wisconsin trout stream. He watched as Jack pulled back hard to set the hook on a rainbow two inches larger than the one he had caught, which also jumped twice before it was gently slid into Jack's net, held firmly between his shortened left arm and body. His rod was placed between his knees as he pulled a hemostat out of an upper pocket and carefully removed the hook from the trout's lip. He slid the net out from under the fish as it was released, and put the fly rod back to work.

It had been a gorgeous morning and was almost noon when Jack and Jimmy met back where they had started. Jimmy had caught seven trout, including an eighteen-inch brown that had attacked the spinner from beneath an undercut. Jack had caught a few more than Jimmy, but his first sixteen-incher had been the biggest he had netted.

Fly was sound asleep, but hadn't slept the whole time as evidenced by a few empty beer bottles and pastry wrappers. His bobber and line were tangled up in a snag along the shore. Jack started to wake him, but stopped himself, whispering to Jimmy that it would be too bad if Fly got skunked. He laid down his rod and jogged along the upstream trail, coming back with a three-pound sucker that had been dead at least a couple days. He followed Fly's line out to the bobber, untangled it, ran the oversized hook through the sucker's tough rubbery lower lip and flipped it out into the swifter current before scrambling back up on the bank.

"That guy's a piece of work," Jimmy observed.

"He's actually not the total idiot he looks like; he has his CPA and works for an accounting firm in Minneapolis." Then Jack turned and said "wake up, Fly, you piece of shit. You got a bite."

Not exactly sure where he was upon waking, Fly saw the pole bending parallel with the ground and jumped up to grab it and start reeling.

"Christ, it's huge," he said, as the dead sucker rolled near the surface twenty yards out. "Fighting like a bastard!"

Fly excitedly started down the bank, only to slip and fall in. Landing on his back and right side, he managed to get completely soaked even though the water was only a foot and a half deep. He kept reeling as the fish skimmed in the last ten feet.

"You really played him out," Jimmy chided.

Reaching for the fish and noticing the empty eye sockets, Fly picked himself up and tried to swing the sucker up the bank at Jack and Jimmy, but in doing so snapped his rod in half.

"Assholes," he muttered as he crawled up the bank on all fours, dragging his broken rod, the tennis-ball-sized bobber and dead sucker behind him.

Two beers later, Fly had gotten over it as Jimmy and Jack washed their sandwiches down with the last two Summits.

"Reminds me of the time we were fishing the dike at Lake Pepin. We were catching a bunch of, ah, what were those again?" Fly asked.

"Striped bass and sheephead," Jack replied.

"Yeah, anyway, these losers come over and started harassing us. They wound up stealing our beer and kicked over our minnow bucket."

Jack, taking over, added, "they grabbed Fly's glasses and were playing keep-away from him. He can only see about six inches without 'em. Looked like Piggy in *Lord of the Flies*. So we finally got his glasses back and decided to take off while they stayed and fished our spot. Knew which car was theirs cause they were really loud when they showed up. So, we picked up a couple of dead sheephead on the way back to throw at their car or something, but then found out they forgot to lock their doors, so we stuffed 'em under the front seat. Hot day too, must have been ninety degrees. I bet they were pissed."

"Served the bastards right," Fly added, punctuating the point by finishing off his beer.

Fly complained the whole way up the hill to the truck as Maggie, who had stayed with Jimmy all morning, followed behind them.

Jack and Fly spent the afternoon at Jimmy's farm. They helped with a few chores after a couple-hour nap. When they had finished the afternoon milking, they decided to stop for pizza on the way back to the Fleet Farm parking lot. They pulled into the Pizza Hut in North Hudson and started on a pitcher of beer while deciding what to order.

"Too bad Kurt isn't here," offered Jack as he filled their glasses, with the head on Fly's rolling over the top and down onto the brown Formica tabletop.

"Yeah, nobody liked pizza more than Kurt," Fly agreed as he lifted the glass and wiped the table beneath it with his shirtsleeve.

Then, turning to Jimmy he said, "back at school there was this farmhouse out in the country where we had a few parties. One night in the winter, on the way back to campus, we slowed down to check out this huge animal along the side of the road... turned out to be a Saint Bernard. When we rolled down the window he came over and stuck his whole head inside the car, slobbering all over the place. Jack opened the back door and he just climbed in... completely filled up the backseat. We wound up naming him Kurt after this fat kid on our floor that had the hairiest back you've ever seen.

'So, we're cruising the dorm with Kurt, and we stop by Grog's room. He'd picked up a frozen pizza on the way home from the farmhouse and had just pulled it out of his toaster oven and was letting it cool down. We asked him for a piece, but he said he was starved and planned on eating the whole thing himself. So Grog goes over to his fridge to get a beer, and Kurt walks over and inhales the whole pizza in two gulps - didn't even chew it. You could see the pizza going through his neck - like a snake eating a rat. Shoulda seen the look on Grog's face - thought he was gonna cry. Of course, Jack and I totally cracked up, and Kurt was one happy pup. We took him back to the farm a couple hours later. Hauled him back to campus a few more times that winter - pretty humorous dog."

The waitress stepped up to the table, pulled out her pad and pen and asked if they were ready to order.

Chapter Four

It was on one of those early summer nights on the patio of Willow Manor, after the train had passed, that Alice told Frank about being born in Clarksville, Missouri on October 25, 1911. She had two older brothers and a younger sister. Their family lived on a houseboat in Black Hills, Missouri, which was where her mother's third cousin, Jessie James, hung out. Her mother had later told her that Jessie, "wasn't as bad as they made him out to be - you know how when somebody gets a reputation, everything gets blamed on 'em."

The Mississippi was, "not near as big as it is now because there was less runoff from farms, and lots of folks lived on the riverbanks." Her father was a fisherman and would row out to the channel in the evening to put his nets out. He went back out in the morning to bring in the nets before rowing downstream to the market. Her mother sewed and cleaned for a dollar a day at a home three miles away, which she walked to every day regardless of the weather.

Most everywhere they went was in a rowboat they kept anchored to the bank by their house, which her father had built up on stilts. There were two rooms - one big room with all the beds in it and another where the kitchen and everything else was kept. They were poor, but so was everyone else, so she didn't know any differently.

The times got hard, so her father went to work at the foundry in Freeport, Illinois, doing ironwork. He later sent for her mother and the kids.

Alice's parents split up when she was six years old, and the state put her and her sister in St. Vincent's Catholic Orphanage in Freeport. The memories from St. Vincent's were not very happy ones. The Catholic sisters were "terribly mean" and used to beat them. They weren't allowed to cry if they got hurt. She remembered having her hair washed several times with kerosene because of head lice. They were not allowed to talk at dinner and had to eat everything on their plate.

She remembered a heavy girl at the end of the table who found a big worm in her cabbage and was told to eat it, or she'd be beaten, so she ate it.

There was a big playground, but they couldn't make any noise, or they would be taken upstairs and beaten. She remembered just holding her sister much of the time and crying. One night Sister Siegfried heard Alice crying for her mother and grabbed her by the arm and dragged her down the hall, locking her in a storage room where she spent the night with nothing but a hard, dusty floor to sleep on.

They had to march, eyes forward, into the classroom. Alice remembered turning around once because a classmate had poked her from behind and getting hit in the face by Sister Siegfried, breaking her nose and splattering blood everywhere.

There was one sister that wasn't like the rest, Sister Clara. She was "the sweetest thing" and would play with them on the playground and would hug them, but she was always looking up into the buildings. Father Smith seemed to like Clara too. Alice remembered Clara getting kind of fat and then disappearing for a few weeks. She was thin again when she came back.

Her father had wanted to keep the kids after her mother left, but the state wouldn't allow it. He still lived in Freeport and got on the good side of the orphanage by doing free stonework for them. He would be around the playground, but they couldn't talk to him. He once sneaked dolls to Alice and her sister for Christmas, but they were promptly taken away.

After two years at the orphanage, she and her sister were allowed a one-day pass to go visit their father at his house. When they got there, all of his stuff was packed up in a tub. They got into Uncle Ed's car and drove down to the docks. They sold the car and bought a big johnboat. On the boat was Alice, her sister, her father, an aunt, a cousin, and Uncle Ed. Her aunt wasn't feeling well so she mostly lay on the bottom of the boat as they rowed down the river.

"The river belonged to nobody; they couldn't even get criminals because authorities couldn't come onto the river to catch folks." They camped on the levees and made a stove out of the washtub and a stovepipe, with a door cut into its side. Alice remembered her aunt cooking biscuits on the tub. The kids "just had a big time 'cause we were free."

Her father and Uncle Ed would fish in the evenings, and in the mornings, they would head downstream again. Alice remembered going through the Keokuk locks, which had been built to allow steamboats to travel upriver. When they got down to Alton, Illinois, they pulled up and camped until her father bought a houseboat for himself and the two girls to live in. Her aunt and uncle had bought a small house up the bank by the railroad tracks. They lived there for three or four years. Somehow, Alice's youngest brother found out they were there and came to live with them. "He was always Daddy's favorite."

Her father got a job at Stone Quarry No. 4, and her brother got one at Quarry No. 1. Life was a lot better for Alice and her sister, but they still missed their mother very much, so her brother came up with a plan. He came home early from the quarry one day and took Alice and her sister down the tracks into town where they took a train back to Freeport and a cab to their oldest brother's house where he lived with his wife, Nellie. All of them took off in his brother's car - an old touring vehicle with window curtains and, "drove and drove" to Sheldon, Wisconsin.

Alice remembered the old muddy road and getting stuck a bunch of times, but they made it to her mother's house on Thanksgiving Day. Her stepfather was just coming from the well and dropped the water pail he was carrying when he saw them. She remembers her mother standing in the doorway - "you can just imagine the welcome we got."

It was a small two-room log cabin, but she remembers "just having a ball." Her mother wrote the orphanage to let them know where the girls were and got approval to keep them. They went to school in Arnold, Wisconsin, and she remembered going to La Crosse one summer. Her mother and stepfather got divorced and he moved to Milwaukee. Alice had grown to love her stepfather very much and went back and forth between the two. Her mother remarried, "a big Indian fella" and moved to Chippewa Falls. Alice married a local guy and they moved to Minneapolis when William got accepted into law school at the University of Minnesota.

Chapter Five

"**D**idn't see you at dinner tonight," Alice offered as Frank wheeled himself next to her on the patio, the sun beginning its final decent toward the horizon.

"Kind of a frustrating day. I went over to Riverview this morning for a bone scan because one of my blood tests made Dr. Sanderson concerned that my prostate cancer has come back. He thinks it might be causing the pain in my left hip. Anyway, they were all set to inject me with this radioactive stuff when they realized that they didn't have insurance authorization yet so I couldn't do the scan. I sat in the hospital lobby for about an hour waiting for the van to come back to get me; must have eaten a half dozen cookies. I just wasn't very hungry when I got back here."

"That's really dumb."

"I know it is, but I got pretty hungry and bored just sitting there with nothing to read but *Redbook* and *People*."

"No, I mean it's really dumb about not having the insurance thing figured out before you went over there."

"Anyway, I'm scheduled for a week from Thursday. Hopefully, it will go smoothly so they can find out what's going on."

"I didn't know you had prostate cancer."

"Yeah, I had surgery about six years ago. They thought they got it all and the blood tests were good - until now. I had pretty much forgotten about it."

"What will they do if the bone scan isn't normal?" Alice asked.

"I don't know. I'll just have to cross that bridge when...."

"*We'll* have to cross that bridge," Alice barged in, a single tear settling just to the left of her nose.

As if on cue, the sun hit the horizon, and the Burlington Northern rumbled by.

"Where do you suppose she'll be come morning?" Frank wondered aloud after the train had passed.

"Albuquerque, New Mexico" Alice responded without hesitation, but with a catch in her voice.

Frank noticed a centipede sitting on the planter next to his wheelchair and pinched it between the thumb and index finger of his left hand. "Watch this," he said as he rolled over to the shallow patio pond on one side of the porch.

"Here, Goldie," he called, tossing the centipede into the water. An eight-inch goldfish came out from under a lily pad to examine and then engulf the bug before darting back to its hideout.

"I didn't know there were fish in there."

"I had Jack pick up three at the pet store last week. They're a little nervous in their new home, but seem to be getting used to it. I got some fish food that I feed 'em and throw in a few bugs for variety."

Pulling herself closer and looking carefully, Alice could see two of the three fish. "What are their names?"

"I just call them all Goldie."

"If you're gonna have pets, they need proper names. Now let's see," she said squinting slightly as she tried to get a better look at the fish in hiding.

The fading sun made it difficult to see the fish well enough to help in naming them, so they decided to put that off until another day. Jack appeared, asked how the fish were doing and helped them back to their rooms.

On the way back to her room Alice noticed Ella Jorgenson in the room next to hers. "Thought you got out of here" she commented, wheeling herself up to Ella's bed.

Ella was eighty-eight, and had been in Willow Manor three months prior while she recovered from a broken right hip. She did well enough to go back to the assisted living center where she had been staying, but then was brought to the hospital by ambulance because she had started passing a large amount of blood rectally. Several tests showed the bleeding was most likely coming from little pockets in the wall of her right colon. Ella got several blood transfusions to replace the blood she had lost and to prepare her for possible surgery.

During her hospital stay, Ella's speech had become garbled, her left arm had become flaccid, and she had lost the ability to swallow as she continued to bleed. The stroke was felt to have been caused, in part, by the drop in blood pressure that accompanied the bleeding. A family conference was held and the issue of whether to put her through surgery was discussed. Nearly all of the family members felt that, with her overall declining health the past couple years, the new stroke, and Ella's stated wish that she have no further operations, surgery shouldn't be done.

The next issue was whether to continue blood transfusions. The doctor had suggested putting a limit as to the number of transfusions she would get and after that let nature take its course. Several family members were concerned about letting Ella "just bleed to death," but in the end agreed to limit the transfusions to two more units of blood. They also talked about whether to place a feeding tube into her stomach for nutrition because of her inability to swallow due to the stroke. The doctor told them they wouldn't have to make that decision for a couple days, but they were all sure that Ella wouldn't want such a tube.

Ella's bleeding would slow down and seem to have stopped, only to show itself again with passage of another liquid maroon stool, having the characteristic smell of blood being broken down by stomach acid.

She received both additional units of blood. That night, when her IV failed, the decision was made not to restart it. The nurse was soon unable to detect a blood pressure and it was decided to stop checking her vital signs. Word got out and relatives and friends started showing up to say goodbye. Her 84-year-old brother would be on the first morning flight from Phoenix, Arizona.

Ella seemed to recognize the voices and understood what was being told to her. She tried to speak, but only an occasional word was intelligible. She did maintain a decent cough and was able to clear her airway when secretions that could not be swallowed got past her vocal cords and started toward her lungs. Her skin was cool and profoundly pale. Her mouth was parched, her eyes sunken and her skin turgor gone. Attempts to give her ice chips by spoon resulted in coughing spells as they went down her windpipe instead of her esophagus. The adjacent waiting room swelled with visitors as the death vigil proceeded.

She took communion at about ten o'clock that night from her pastor of over forty years.

But she didn't die that night or the next week. The bleeding stopped and her speech and swallowing gradually improved. She was allowed to stay in the hospital longer than usually allowed because the medical staff felt her death was imminent. She stayed in the same hospital room, but was taken care of by hospice volunteers so that hospital expense could be lessened.

Visitors still came by but with decreasing frequency. Ella knew why they were coming and told Alice that she had tried to die, but just couldn't. She had even tried holding her breath. It finally became apparent that her death was no longer as imminent as they had thought, and she was transferred back to Willow Manor. She was still not able to take much nutrition by mouth and was very weak. The doctor had told the family that she was at high risk of developing pneumonia and, if she did, she would have a tough time fighting it off. Considering her overall situation he had told them if she did get pneumonia, he would talk to the family before bringing her back to the hospital or even starting antibiotics.

Two of Ella's daughters had come by with her belongings and gotten her settled in before they went back to their own homes. It had been a very difficult and tiring week for them, including making initial plans for a funeral that didn't happen.

Alice spent about fifteen minutes talking with Ella, her crippled hands on Ella's bruised and swollen hands, looking into the milky lenses of her cataract-ridden eyes.

"Are you in any pain?" Alice asked.

"No... but...."

"But what?"

"I don't mind the days, but I get kind of scared at night," she said in slurred, but very understandable speech.

"Even when you were at home?"

"Not as much as this past week."

"Would you like me to stay with you tonight?"

"Oh, you can't do that."

"Of course I can. Let me go to my room and clean up some. I'll be right back."

Alice spent that night at Ella's bedside, with the bathroom light on so it wouldn't be totally dark. In the morning they had breakfast together in Ella's room before Alice went back to her own room to catch up on lost sleep. She recruited Frank to help keep Ella company at night.

Over the next two weeks her eating never really picked up and she became weaker and less responsive. Her cough worsened as pneumonia set in and the decision was made to not treat it; as a result, her room was placed off limits to the other residents.

Ella died on a bright afternoon with summer rays streaming in the window and three generations of family at her bedside, her two daughters already replanning the funeral.

Chapter Six

"Where's Alice tonight?" Jack asked as he joined Frank on the porch.

"Oh, I told her I was worn out from my trip to the clinic today and was going to bed early. She said she was tired too and was going to read for a while and then go to bed herself. I just came out to get some fresh air."

"What did the doctor say? Weren't you supposed to get some test results back today?"

"Yeah, both the repeat bone scan and the PSA looked bad."

"Did you tell Alice?"

"No, I told her the results weren't back yet," Frank responded.

"Now what? Any different treatments or anything?"

"Maybe. The urologist is coming by tomorrow to talk about it. Didn't sound very good. I'm going to see a naturopath next week to find out about anything else I might be able to try."

"Oh, where is that?" Jack asked.

"In St. Paul, got the name from a guy that farms out by us. He says his cousin had a bad cancer with six months to live, got put on a mega-vitamin program and is still alive five years later. You know much about that stuff?"

"Not really, but one of the nurses here is working on a master's thesis looking at alternative treatments for cancer. Western medicine has been slow to adopt treatments for all kinds of diseases that have been used in other parts of the world. Her biggest problem with many of them is, if they work, they should be able to show that they are effective in a scientific fashion, similar to the trials that other treatments go through. There are a lot of natural extracts, like Taxol from the Japanese yew, that are currently being used for treating cancer and other diseases. Some of the alternative treatments she found were just plain silly, like fruit juice or coffee enemas. Cancer patients are probably the most vulnerable of all consumers and even level-headed people, will buy into stuff they normally would laugh at if it gives them any glimmer of hope."

Jack continued, "She found a guy from town with metastatic melanoma who spent two weeks and $15,000 at an alternative treatment ranch in Colorado getting various enemas and lymphatic brushings where they rubbed his body twice a day with coarse brushes to stimulate his immune system. Developed these weeping sores all over his body that they told him were dead tumor cells being shed. Comes home thinking he was cured, but his wife noticed that his speech was slurred. CT of his head showed big mets in his brain. He died three weeks later.

'My dad spent $150 on what was basically shredded alfalfa to treat his pancreatic cancer. He felt pretty foolish when he realized he'd been taken, but the brother of somebody's cousin had supposedly been cured by it.

'There was a time when terminal cancer patients flocked to Mexico for laetrile, you know... apricot pits. Who talks about that stuff anymore?

"What about that mega-vitamin thing he was talking about?" Frank asked.

"I don't know much about the mega-vitamin thing, but you need to be skeptical. Our body's immune system can help fight off cancers like it does with infections. It usually does better with a good diet, sleep and some exercise. Relaxation techniques like meditation and massage can help, and a positive attitude may be the most important of all." Jack said.

"Well, I think I'll go anyway just to see what they have to say," said Frank.

"Just be careful about writing too big a check without knowing what you're getting," Jack warned.

"I won't be needing the money much longer anyway the way it sounds. So what difference does it make?"

"It's your life and your money. I just hate to see people make money off folks who are grasping at straws. If you want to give away your money, there are probably better choices," Jack said.

The next day was Saturday, and Frank hung around his room waiting for Dr. Storley to stop by. When he had called the clinic to make an appointment with his urologist the nurse told him that Dr. Storley was going to be at Willow Manor on Saturday to see another patient and could stop by his room.

The late August morning was unseasonably cool, which was Frank's kind of weather; mid-sixties, sunny with a light breeze and with the maples still a month away from beginning their fall pageantry. As Frank daydreamed out the window his attention was directed to the playground across the parking lot. Two young boys were having the "my dad's bigger, stronger, faster, tougher than your dad" argument. One of the boys appeared to be losing the battle and came back with, "well, my dad's a urologist, and he'll cut your dad's pecker right off." The other boy didn't seem to know what a urologist was, but clearly understood the rest of it and the argument was over. Frank relayed the conversation to Dr. Storley when he came in.

"I'm surprised he even knows what I do. The kid's totally unimpressed that I went to college or medical school or residency, but I'll tell ya, the day I rented a bobcat to push dirt around the yard... that day I was pretty big in his eyes."

Dr. Storley was relaxed and easy to talk to as he sat on the edge of the bed where he could peek out the window to check on his son. He explained that prostate cancer was stimulated by testosterone and that removal of the testicles was a way to slow down the growth of the cancer. He also said that medications were available to do essentially the same thing and were nearly as effective although very expensive and had potential side effects.

The decision not to have the surgery was an easy one for Frank. They found a common ground in that Dr. Storley had grown up in Wisconsin and they both felt the Pack was definitely back and heading for the Super Bowl if Favre could stay healthy.

After leaving a note on Frank's chart Dr. Storley moved quickly toward the exit, remembering the lengthy list of errands he had yet to do before being home by two o'clock when his wife had to leave for a baby shower and he himself had to shuttle kids to dance practice, Cub Scouts, bowling, and a birthday party.

That morning he had left at six o'clock to begin patient rounds and charting at three hospitals and two nursing homes. His wife had gotten their son Joe to hockey practice and their daughter Katie and other son Kent to soccer games. He had picked up Joe on his way between hospitals.

Dr. Storley was stopped in the hall by Arnie Galowitz, an elderly fellow he had done an endoscopic prostate surgery on a while back for enlargement of the prostate, which caused him trouble urinating. He remembered Arnie had lived for most of his life on Daggert Lake, in the Cross Lake chain of northern Minnesota, and that Arnie's wife had spent so much time fishing off their dock that Arnie had wired a telephone line down to it so he could call his wife up for meals. They had bought the seven acres of shorefront property thirty-five years earlier for $600, and had sold it for $150,000 when his wife's health had begun declining. They had used the money to buy a comfortable townhouse in White Bear Lake with an annual association fee to cover all maintenance. It had seemed like an ideal place to retire, but Arnie's wife had died three months after they moved, and he found himself all alone and in declining health. Recovering from surgery for a broken hip, Arnie found Willow Manor to be a friendly place with more chances for socializing than at his townhouse in a neighborhood of strangers.

Arnie had been a bosun's mate with the 4th Platoon of Company A in the 8th U.S. Naval Construction Battalion during the invasion of Iwo Jima in February of 1943. He had been offshore when the Marines went in to secure the island and had come ashore with his company shortly afterward to construct airstrips and establish a water supply. They had cleared the strips with bulldozers after filling in the pockmarked, post-bombing landscape. The legendary battle had been intense, and he had been back on ship with a clear view of Mount Suribachi when the American flag had been raised.

"We were sure glad to see Old Glory go up. It had been touch and go for a while, but when we saw the flag, we knew we had 'er.'" He had also seen the second flag raising, which had been ordered to obtain the now-famous picture that immortalized the moment.

After securing the island, the Marines had left the Seabees to occupy the base, and Arnie had stayed on the island until he was discharged from the military in November of that year.

The Japanese had an elaborate system of caves and underground shelters. During the fighting, many Marines had lost their lives investigating caves by getting a bayonet in the back from a Japanese soldier on a ledge inside the mouth of the cave. This had led the Marines to use flame-throwers and grenades to clear out the caves before going in. Not all of the Japanese soldiers had been found.

Arnie remembered standing in chow line for breakfast at 0600 one morning in June or July when two disheveled Japanese soldiers that had been holed up just five hundred feet from the U.S. barracks since February had come out of nowhere with a white flag and surrendered. After wolfing down breakfast, they revealed the entrance to a large, concealed cave that led to the surrender of sixteen additional Japanese soldiers.

"Hey, Doc, friend of mine named Bob pulled into a gas station over in White Bear and sees a sign that says, 'Free chance at sex with every fill-up.' So he fills up his car with gas and asks the owner, 'Say, what's the deal with the free chance at sex with every fill-up.' The owner tells him to pick a number between one and ten. Bob picks seven. Owner says the number was eight, 'just off by one' and that Bob should come back and try again. So the next week Bob is riding around in his friend's car when his friend notices he's low on gas, so Bob tells him about the place with the free chance at sex with every fill-up. Bob's friend drives over to the station, fills up his tank, and asks the owner about the free chance at sex. Owner tells him to pick a number between one and ten. Bob's friend picks three. Owner says, 'Sorry, but the number was two' and that he should come back and try again.

"As they're driving out of the station, Bob says, 'Man, we were both so close. I bet we get it next time.' Bob's friend tells him, 'Hey, Bob, I think it's just a gimmick to get people to buy more gas. I don't think there is any free sex.' Bob says, 'Oh, yeah, there is, last week my wife won twice.'"

"I think that's the station my wife has been going to," Dr. Storley said, discreetly glancing at the clock on the wall above Arnie's head and in a softer voice, "Don't forget that Nurse Schwartz still has the hots for you."

"I know, but I'm holding out for a younger one."

"All right, Arnie, take care of yourself."

On the way out, Dr. Storley passed several other residents who were not nearly as with it as Arnie, who either sat expressionless or reached out toward him with uncoordinated movements and started in on nonsensical conversations or demands, which he ignored. It was almost noon, and he had barely enough time to do the errands on the list he pulled from his pocket, which included picking up dry cleaning, dog food, light bulbs, furnace filters, assorted groceries, and propane for the grill, renewing vehicle license tabs, and getting a birthday present for an 11-year-old boy.

As he stepped out of Willow Manor into the bright sunshine, he noticed how fresh and crisp the air smelled, and he took in the vibrancy of the moment. His son and friend were swinging to a height nearly to the top beam of the swing set, so they would drop in a couple-second free fall on their way down before the chain links would tighten abruptly and resume the arc. There was youthful excitement in their eyes and voices as he watched them and listened to their unrestrained and flowing thoughts on the Packers and Vikings, the girls in their class, the fun they had at the sleepover at Jake's house last weekend, and the fun they would have at Jordan's birthday party that afternoon.

Dr. Storley glanced back through the glass doors into Willow Manor at the residents who had followed him to the exit, then at his watch, and decided he had enough time to throw the football around in the park across the street for a few minutes before starting on the list of errands. This idea was met with "I get to be Brett Favre," and "Go ahead, I get to be John Randall, and I'll have you for lunch."

The ball was pulled out of the back end of the Storley's forest green Explorer, and the three jogged across the street to the park. Two kids from their class were already in the park kicking a soccer ball around and came over as soon as they saw the football. Other kids appeared from behind hedgerows and playground structures, and soon a five-against-five, two-hand touch game was underway with Dr. Storley quarterbacking both teams and with his tan argyle socks and brown loafers marking the four corners of the field, his navy-blue blazer hanging off the teeter totter.

Dr. Storley had been a high school quarterback and had the boys running some of the same routes his high school receivers had run. The invigorating day had him feeling like Joe Montana as he dodged the no-count rushers and picked out his receivers. The half hour long game conveniently ended in a tie as the exhausted kids flopped onto the ground and rehashed the game's highlights.

Nelson's dairy store caught Dr. Storley's eye across the street on the other side of the park.

"Anybody up for ice cream?" All ten kids were on their feet before the words left his mouth, and they were on their way, running short pass routes as they went. The store was well known for its great ice cream and equally well known for being understaffed. Dr. Storley and the boys piled into the back of the store behind fifteen or so other customers waiting to be served by two employees, scooping ice cream at a deliberate pace. When their turn came, Superman flavor, a multi-colored confection tasting like plain vanilla in a waffle cone, was the most popular choice with Dr. Storley opting for a root-beer float.

They crossed back to the park and sat on the side of a small hill in the shade of 100-year-old oaks to savor their choices. Dr. Storley looked back toward Willow Manor and then at the ten boys around his feet, ice cream dripping off their chins and onto already filthy t-shirts and jerseys. He didn't bother looking at his watch because it really didn't matter. As the other kids finished their ice cream and filtered off, he and Joe started back across the park toward the Willow Manor parking lot.

"Dad, that was really fun. Thanks... but I think you're gonna be in trouble when we get home."

"We're gonna need a really good excuse."

"How about telling Mom that some guy had a chainsaw accident and cut his pecker off, and you had to sew it back on."

"Gee, why does that sound familiar?" he asked, reminding himself that he had meant to talk to Joe about the conversation Frank had overheard. He decided to let it go for now. "That might be a little too dramatic. How about we just tell her I had to treat somebody with a stone blocking their kidney."

"Boring."

The car ride home was spent planning on how they could still get everybody where they needed to go and at least get some of the errands done. After dropping his brother and sister off, they could pick up the birthday present on the way to the party and wrap it in the car. Dr. Storley would then have an hour to run errands before he had to start picking kids up again.

"No problem," Dr. Storley summarized.

"Piece of cake," Joe agreed.

"Name the band," Dr. Storley said as he turned up the radio and began tapping on the steering wheel, mouthing the words to "Radar Love."

"Golden Earring," Joe responded without hesitation.

"Glad to see you're listening to something other than that hip hop rap crap."

"Only when I ride around with you."

"Just want to make sure you're learning your three Rs (reading, writing and rock-n-roll)."

"That's four Rs."

"Rock 'n' roll only counts for one."

"What about arithmetic?"

"Do you have a calculator?" asked Dr. Storley.

"Yeah," Joe replied.

"Know how to use it?"

"Yeah."

"So what do you need to know arithmetic for?"

"Dad, Mom's a math teacher."

"Don't tell her I said that. Just keep studying so you can be a toad scholar someday."

"What's a toad scholar?" asked Joe.

Dr. Storley answered, "You get to hop directly from high school to CEO of a major corporation like Microsoft. It'll save your mom and me a lot of college tuition money."

"You're so full of shit."

"Hand me the bar of soap in the glove department."

"That's compartment," Joe corrected.

"Whatever. Just remember that the 70s were the golden decade for music."

"Yeah, and 'Freebird' was the greatest song ever written and '*Machine Head*' was the greatest album."

"You got it."

"But then that's also the opinion of a guy who grew up in Wisconsin, thinks cheddarwurst is a gourmet food, and tried to moonwalk in the kitchen to that Michael Jackson song 'Billie Jean.'"

"Wasn't me."

"I've got it on video tape," Joe said, teasing his father.

"Anybody sees that, you're dead meat," Dr. Storley jokingly threatened his son.

"Just keep that tape in mind when my birthday comes around."

"That's extortion."

"That's life; deal with it," said Joe.

When they got home, the two-tone brown Dodge Caravan was not in the garage, and Jill and the other kids were gone. A note on the kitchen counter read, *"Took Katie to dance on my way to the shower. She'll get a ride home with the Andersons. Kent is at Will's house. They'll take him to bowling, but you need to pick him up at five o'clock. The birthday party is at 4 o'clock, and Joe still needs a present. We had talked about getting a golf-ball retriever. They're on sale at Target. We're having grilled pork chops for dinner so don't forget the propane. Love J."*

Dr. Storley pulled the errand list out of his pocket and added, "florist" to the bottom.

Chapter Seven

Frank had gotten used to the idea of being in a nursing home and realized that Jimmy wouldn't be able to take care of him and the farm. The nurses appreciated his wit and good nature, and would often tease or flirt with him. He got to know many of them quite well and found himself frequently counseling, consoling, or just listening to troubles concerning husbands, boyfriends, kids, cars, or finances.

Many of the nurses lived across the river in Wisconsin, and most of those were avid Green Bay Packer fans. For balance, there was about an equal number of nurses who were Minnesota Vikings fans, although not nearly as vocal or committed.

Once the NFL season got going, Sunday afternoons were the liveliest time of the week at Willow Manor. Two televisions would be set up in the lobby; number boards would be organized, and popcorn popped. Many of the residents would be wearing jerseys or stocking caps of either Vikings' purple or Packers' green and gold. Some knew what all the fuss was about; most didn't, but even those who could no longer tell a football from a hockey puck seemed to enjoy the sense of something exciting going on.

Frank had lived in Wisconsin the last forty-seven years and remembered well the Lombardi days. He still remembered, to a man, the starting lineup from the 1966 championship game against Baltimore. His enthusiasm for the game had mellowed, but he was still proud to be from a state where a small market team could be owned by its fans and compete with the mega-market teams.

Alice's husband had been a Vikings fan since they had come into the league as an expansion team in 1964. He had forty-yard-line seats at the old Metropolitan Stadium where Bud Grant's expressions on the sidelines were as frozen as the turf they played on.

Although Alice wasn't a big fan of football, she had to admit those days had been fun. They would always go to the stadium parking lot a couple of hours early to tailgate before the games, and she would sneak in a half-pint of snowshoe grog or peppermint schnapps to "keep the pipes open" as the temperature dropped. She herself remembered many of the players - Joe Kapp and Bill Brown being her favorites. But she also remembered the intimidating big-play defense led by Carl Eller, Jim Marshall, and Alan Page.

She met Alan Page at an attorney's social event years later, after he had retired from football and had begun his law practice. His playing weight had been around two-hundred-eighty pounds, and she was surprised to see how thin he looked at two-hundred-twenty pounds.

On the first Sunday in September, the Packers and Vikings opened their regular seasons by playing each other. Frank and Alice decided to watch the game in Frank's room. Alice pulled out an old Vikings sweater she hadn't worn since William had died, but it had been packed with her clothes and sent along to Willow Manor by her daughters. Frank only had his Packer's stocking hat to wear, being somewhat envious of the cheese-wedge hats a few of the nurses were wearing. The anticipation of the afternoon's game brought them back to a time when their bodies had been as healthy as their minds.

By game time, Alice's stuffed chair and Frank's wheelchair were in position, and they had a tray of snacks and sodas with Frank topping off his Pepsi with a bit of brandy from the lower drawer.

It was in the third quarter of that game that Frank picked out his future granddaughter-in-law. Kelly was one of a couple of nurses who came around hawking hot dogs as a vendor would, except they were free. She was five years out of nursing school and had worked at the University of Minnesota Hospital before coming to Willow Manor, where she was allowed to work flexible hours while working on her master's degree in Nursing Administration. She had been Frank's nurse on numerous occasions and had watched his progress since he had first been admitted.

Kelly looked to be around 5'8", with dark brown hair that fell softly to her mid-back. Despite her busy schedule, she supported a healthy late summer tan and always had a sparkle in her brown eyes. She tended to wear less traditional nursing attire than most of the other nurses, and was wearing a yellow sundress as she came by Frank's room with the tray of hot dogs and condiments.

Alice and Frank each ordered one; and as Kelly leaned over in front of Frank with the ketchup, he found himself staring at the most perfect set he had ever seen. He had the dual sense of appreciation from an aesthetic standpoint, and a deeper sensation he hadn't felt for quite some time. He didn't know if he would have appreciated the moment any less if he had gone ahead with the surgery, but at least for that moment was glad he hadn't.

Frank immediately stepped up the conversation with Kelly, having a great deal of interest in her master's program, her hometown of Edina, and anything else she had to say. He also found out that she had recently broken up with a guy she had gone out with for less than a year.

"Well, if it's not going to work out, no sense in prolonging it," Frank had consoled her, deciding right there she was the perfect girl for Jimmy.

Alice caught the whole show and cracked up with laughter as Kelly left the room. Frank, realizing he'd been caught, played as though he didn't know what she was laughing about as a sheepish grin crept across his face. For Frank, the rest of the game, won by the Packers 16 to 10, was spent planning how he could get Kelly and his grandson together.

Kelly's tan had briefly faded the previous weekend while changing Billy Backstrom's foot dressing. Billy was a 67-year-old diabetic whose only real hobby was smoking cigarettes. He had been seen weekly at at his apartment by a visiting nurse who checked his blood sugar, blood pressure, pulse, and temperature, listened to his heart and lungs, and made sure he was taking his medications. While asking him a few general questions, Billy mentioned that his left foot had turned "kind of blue."

Taking off his shoe and sock, she found that the skin over half his foot and two toes was coal black. The next day Billy had seen his family doctor in the morning and a vascular surgeon in the afternoon. The surgeon had given him the option of going straight to an amputation, which might have to be above the knee because of bad circulation, or trying to save the foot. Despite his sub-optimal existence, Billy lived independently and felt that an amputation would jeopardize that independence. He was willing to go along with whatever was necessary to save the foot including trying to quit smoking.

The day after seeing the surgeon, Billy had an angiogram which showed a severe narrowing of the main artery to the left leg within the pelvis, and a complete blockage of the artery just above his knee. In addition, two of the three smaller arteries carrying oxygenated blood to his feet were blocked. The radiologist doing the angiogram had opened the pelvic artery with an expandable titanium cylinder, which had been passed from the right groin where they had accessed the arterial system to do the angiogram. The following week he had undergone a vascular bypass from his left groin to just below his knee using vein from the inner aspect of the leg to carry the blood around the obstruction.

After the bypass had been completed most of the dead tissue on his left foot had been cut away and dressings placed. The plan was to place a skin graft when the wound was cleaner. The hospital's no-smoking rule had motivated him to a quick recovery, and three days later he was at Willow Manor getting whirlpool treatments three times per week and daily dressing changes on the open sores on his left foot. The sores were improving, but remained a bit foul smelling with persistent dead tissue in a couple of spots. He had been back to see his surgeon in clinic where some of the dead tissue had been surgically removed. Willow Manor had a no-smoking policy inside, but had a smoking patio for the residents, which Billy still frequented as often as possible.

During one of the smoking breaks, a fly must have gotten inside his foot dressings, for on Sunday morning when Kelly had unwrapped the gauze, she was greeted by a couple of dozen squirming white maggots crawling over the open wounds. The wounds themselves had never looked better, with much of the remaining dead tissue having been devoured by the ravenous larvae.

Chapter Eight

Jimmy washed down the last couple bites of his New York strip
with the last couple inches of his Michelob Golden Draft, while
Kelly finished half her roughy and took a sip of chardonnay. They
watched the shadowy trees and distant lights out of the train window as it slowed to a halt, shuddered, and started back the way it had
come.

Frank had made dinner train reservations for him and Alice, and
had hired Kelly as a private nurse - for $20 an hour - to go along for
assistance. The nursing home van had brought them to the train
station where Jimmy was waiting for them. He remembered Kelly
from Willow Manor, but didn't know her name and didn't bother
introducing himself as he helped Kelly lower first Alice's and then
Frank's wheelchair from the van to the asphalt parking lot.

Frank's introductions brought little response from Jimmy or Kelly as they pushed Frank and Alice toward the station. Frank pulled four tickets out of his burgundy sport jacket pocket as they wheeled over to the boarding stairs. They had gotten Alice and Frank situated in their window booth, with Alice facing up track to the north and Frank down track.

As Jimmy and Kelly looked for their seats, Frank stopped them and said, "I think your table is upstairs."

Jimmy hadn't noticed there was an upstairs level, but he and Kelly checked their tickets, found the stairs, and found their table which was almost directly above the table where Frank and Alice sat, with Kelly facing up track and Jimmy down. They both had watched out the window at the station as the last of the passengers boarded. The silence was broken as their waitress asked them if they wanted anything from the bar. Jimmy only had a couple of bucks with him and hesitated until the waitress mentioned their bill would be on his grandfather's tab. He ordered a beer, and Kelly asked for a glass of chardonnay, as the train slowly pulled out of the station and started north through the woods on the west bank of the St. Croix River.

Most of the trip north and west was spent looking out the window and eating their food, which Kelly thought was surprisingly good considering that everyone got served at the same time.

Kelly had worked three-to-elevens and nights much of the summer, which allowed her a lot of time outside, even with her studies, resulting in the healthy tan that matched her brown eyes and complimented her brown hair, which had been lightened by the same sun that had darkened her skin. Jimmy brought his gaze into the train long enough to notice Kelly's lustrous eyes, and then the unfinished roughy on her plate. On cue, Kelly said she was full and asked him if he wanted the rest.

"Yeah, sure, how is it?"

"Perfect," she said, lifting her plate and gently pushing it on to his. "Frank says you do a lot of fishing. What else do you like to do?"

"Drive around in my truck listening to the radio with my lab, Maggie."

Silence followed as Jimmy finished the roughy and signaled to the waitress for another beer.

"What kind of music do you like?" Kelly asked, trying to keep the conversation going.

"Metallica, Nirvana, Pearl Jam, some oldies like Dylan...." Then he said more quietly as he looked down the aisle to see if the waitress was coming, "Planted a black walnut tree on a grassy hill down by our pond last spring after Cobain killed himself."

Kelly had also been affected by the tragic loss of a resonant voice for the post-boomer dreams and despairs.

More silence.

"Any favorite Dylan songs?" Kelly asked.

"Oh, I like the poetry of 'Tangled up in Blue,'" replied Jimmy.

"There was music in the cafes at night and revolution in the air."

"Yep," Jimmy said as his beer arrived along with the dessert cart. Kelly chose the raspberry tart and ordered another chardonnay, while Jimmy picked the turtle cheesecake.

"Read much?" Kelly continued.

"I can if that's what you're asking," he said, taking a swallow of beer as he looked out the window again.

"Don't get defensive. I was just wondering what you liked to read."

"Oh, *Field and Stream, Road and Track,* Thoreau and Emerson."

Mouth open, about to take a bite of tart, Kelly put the fork down and looked up as Jimmy shoveled in a generous bite of cheesecake.

"The first two I expected, but I didn't picture you as the Norwegian bachelor philosopher."

Unamused, "I'm actually mostly Irish with a little Swedish, and I just like the way they both used the natural world to explain the man-made world. Einstein said to understand everything better we should 'look deep, deep into nature.' Emerson and Thoreau did that.

Emerson compared our society to a wave, saying the wave moves forward, but the stuff of which it is composed does not. I think that's true. I look at the advances we've made in science and technology the past couple generations, but I don't see that our generation is made up of folks more advanced than Frank's; in some ways we may have slid back a bit."

"And Thoreau?"

"When I was in Boy Scouts, the goal of our five-mile hike was just to get from A to B so we could check it off toward our next merit badge. When Thoreau went hiking, or 'sauntering' as he called it, he was guided by brooks, ravines, crests, his heart; he didn't have a predetermined route to restrict his curiosities. Many of his most rewarding hikes ended close to where they had started. That's the way I prefer to hike and, I suppose, to live."

"Like living alone on a dairy farm, unable to go anywhere because the cows need to be milked twice a day?"

Ignoring her question, he said, "I don't think most people spend enough time by themselves to have any real thoughts of their own. They end up getting programmed by the media and marketing folks. They let the talking heads tell them what they think about stuff."

"What else don't you like?" Kelly pressed on now that she had him talking.

A large swallow of beer preceded his answer as Jimmy tried to remember the last time he had been asked this many questions. "Being in a social situation where you have to make a lot of phony conversation with people you don't really know or have much in common with."

"Like tonight?" Kelly bit back.

"No, what I mean is, I know who my best friends are cause they're the ones I can sit in a boat with all day, and we can go hours without saying a word and not feel uncomfortable about it. If you have something to say, you say it; otherwise you just fish.

'My old girlfriend couldn't understand that. We had some friends who had gotten married and were splitting up. I went fishing with the guy, who happened to be my best friend since we were little kids. We spent the whole day together and never talked about the split. I figured if he wanted to talk about it, he would have brought it up.

'Anyway, that night my girlfriend stopped by to get the scoop on what was going on between them, and I didn't have anything new to tell her. She got really pissed off and told me that Cal and I both had a problem with communication and that I was going to have as much trouble with relationships as Cal did. Maybe she was right. Cal's divorced now, and I haven't really had a steady girlfriend since she and I broke up."

Kelly eased back into her seat. "Doesn't it get kind of boring or lonely, spending so much time by yourself on the farm?"

"I do quite a bit of taxidermy in the winter."

"How did you get started on that?"

"Took a mail order course from the Northwestern School of Taxidermy that I found in an Outdoor Life magazine. Ordered the hard foam bodies and glass eyes from Van Dyke's in Woonsocket South Dakota. I liked doing ducks and pheasants 'cuz you can really fluff up their plumage and make 'em look good. Mammals were tougher for me to make look natural but squirrels were fun to put in goofy poses and I did a roadkill badger that turned out pretty good.

'My best mount was probably a snowy owl that got hit by a car and was in perfect shape. It was a year when the lemming population in northern Canada was way down and a lot of snowies came south looking for food. They are used to being on the tundra so they were flying low and landing on roads. That's why a lot of 'em were hit by cars. You can't keep live or dead birds of prey so I donated the mount to our high school biology department."

'But, yeah, sometimes it gets a little boring, like the morning I spray painted 'Metallica Rules' on the side of a Holstein. I figured Frank would be pissed at me for messing with his cows, so I tried to wash it off and couldn't. That night Frank went out to the barn for something, and on the way back he looked out in the pasture, and there was the Holstein looking like a billboard on the Interstate. He came back and didn't say a word. So, next morning I was in the barn milking, half asleep, and I was hooking one up, and I noticed 'Benny' in big, spray-painted letters on the cow's side. I looked around, and there was a 'Glen' and a 'Mitch' too. I started laughing so hard I had to sit down - thinking of that silly old bastard stumbling around in the pasture with a flashlight and a can of spray paint after I went to bed."

"It's too bad about the stroke."

"Yeah... shit happens, I guess."

Chapter Nine

J immy's thoughts went back to those first days in the hospital when the doctors weren't sure Frank would live - two days on the respirator with a care conference to talk over the situation, and plant the seed that at some point it might be best to just pull the plug. But Frank had rallied and had gotten the breathing tube out. He had the feeding tube put into his stomach before going to the nursing home. It would be a couple more weeks before he could speak.

Jimmy hated going to visit him. He hated seeing Frank that way, hated the smell of the place - old twisted demented bodies in wheelchairs scattered about the place, drooling on themselves, clawing at him as he walked past them.

The second time he went to visit, he told Frank that he had to get him out of there - somehow, they could manage at home. He just couldn't let him stay in that shit hole. It would kill him for sure when he woke up and realized where he was.

As much as he hated going there, Jimmy visited at least once a day. He'd talk to Frank about the farm, the weather, fishing, whatever, and he started noticing that Frank was paying more attention, moving his eyes more, turning his head, making more effort to speak. Jimmy kept on talking because other than a sister he had lost contact with, Frank was the only family that he had. He got to know the nurses, and his appreciation grew for the care they gave Frank and the difficulty of their jobs, not hesitating or complaining as they cleaned up involuntary bowel movements, washed and combed his hair, shaved him, brushed his teeth, hooked up the tube feedings, moved him from side to side to prevent bed sores, talked to him, encouraged him. The physical therapist did range-of-motion exercises and worked on his speaking and swallowing.

Jimmy noticed the placard by the chart rack in the nurses' workroom: *"Opportunity - I shall pass through this world but once. Any good therefore that I can do or any kindness that I can show to any human being, let me do it now; let me not defer or neglect it, for I shall not pass this way again."* He begrudgingly realized that, at least for now, this was the best place for Frank.

Jimmy also got to know a few of the other residents who, despite their physical or mental impairments, weren't the total vegetables he had initially thought they were.

"Enough of that. What do you like to do?" Jimmy asked.

"Ski, rollerblade, go to movies and plays, listen to music."

"What do you like to listen to?" he asked, trying to keep the shoe on the other foot.

"Depends. If I go out with the girls, we'll usually find some place with a head banger playing, but at home or in the car I mostly listen to jazz."

"Best concert?"

"Funnest was Jimmy Buffet at Red Rock," Kelly answered.

"Parrothead, huh?"

"I guess," she said.

"Where do you ski?" Jimmy continued.

"Around here. I mostly go to Afton. Our family used to go to Vail every winter, but I haven't been out West for a couple of years...I really miss those back bowls. How about you, ski at all?"

"I started snowboarding a couple of years ago. Mostly just go up to Trollhaugen. They've got a snowboard park that's pretty cool."

"I've been there. You don't really seem like the snowboarding type. How'd you get into that?"

"Frank used to pull me around with the tractor in the winter on some old wooden skis. He took me up there downhill skiing a few times. Rented a snowboard one afternoon and haven't gone back to regular skis since."

A philosopher and a shredder, Kelly observed to herself, finishing her chardonnay, having milked that avenue of conversation as far as it was going to go.

Jimmy finished his beer and turned his attention outside the train to the fading light and early October hardwoods, looking down the tracks to see if they were almost back to the station.

The silence was tough on Kelly. "Any interest in poetry or writing?"

"Some," Jimmy replied, expanding no further.

"Well, which one?" The wine was beginning to put just a touch of slur in her words.

"Both, I guess," - again going no further.

"You know any good poems by heart?" Kelly asked.

"Yeah."

"How about one that goes with a nice meal on a dinner train?"

"There's a short one by Robert Service I like," Jimmy replied

"Robert Service? Didn't he write that Sam McGee poem?"

"'The Cremation of Sam McGee'?" guessed Jimmy.

"Yeah, we used to read that around the campfire when I was a counselor at Y camp."

"He's probably best known for that one and 'The Men That Don't Fit In,' but I like some of his other stuff better."

"Well, go ahead."

"Just think some night the stars will gleam," he began with Kelly liking the start and leaning forward.

Upon a cold gray stone

and trace a name with silver beam

and lo, twill be your own.

That night is speeding on

to greet your epitaphic rhyme.

Your life is but a little beat

within the heart of time.

A little pain, a little gain,

a laugh lest you may moan.

A little fame, a little blame,

a star gleam on a stone.

"That's awful," she said, pulling back in her seat.

"What do you mean?" he asked, restraining a smile.

"What do I mean?" she asked. "You tell me a poem about stars shining on my gravestone and wonder why I don't like it. It makes our life on earth seem so... so insignificant," she commented, as the middle three syllables slurred together.

"A more positive way of looking at the poem is that what is insignificant is most of the stuff people get so bent out of shape about because, in the scope of things, most of it really doesn't matter. But you're right in that our time here is 'a short journey from nothingness to nothingness,' as Hemingway put it. What's seventy or eighty years in the life history of a planet? We have some good moments and some bad ones, with a lot of filler in between. You try to create as many good ones as possible and savor the piss out of 'em when they come.'

'And, you find ways to keep the bad ones from getting you down too much. For some folks, the good moments come from raising kids, helping people, or trying to leave the world a better place than they found it. Either way, you gotta hope that by the time you get in Frank's situation, you have something good to look back on, 'cause there's not a lot to look forward to. I think Frank would trade all his tomorrows for a single yesterday."

"Well Janis, I'm not so sure he would, but I do think you're what's keeping him going right now just like a lot of the older folks who get great enjoyment out of their kids and grandkids along with activities, hobbies, and travel they didn't have time for when they were younger."

"More like it's Alice that's keeping him going." Jimmy said.

"He also has eternal life in heaven to look forward to."

"I think the poem was just about life on earth," he said, trying not to go down that road.

"Do you think there is a heaven?" she asked, pinning him down.

"I don't know. The whole idea of a Creator and a heaven seem pretty far-fetched, but I also haven't heard any scientist come up with an explanation for where all the matter in the universe came from. I mean, there had to be a beginning where something came from nothing, and I don't think anything I learned in high school physics explains that. Sure, heaven is beyond comprehension, but so are light years and black holes and a couple strands of DNA becoming a Mozart or an Einstein or a girl with such beautiful eyes as...." He stopped himself and turned his attention outside the train as he wondered how that had slipped out.

Surprised, she looked at his reflection in the window and said, "They actually are getting close to figuring out the whole DNA thing, how those little strands work and how they can be cloned or changed. Most of the mystery will probably be gone a decade or so from now."

"Yeah, I suppose it will."

Kelly, changing the subject, asked, "Do you think you've had more good moments or bad?"

The memories of his mother's death in a car accident, where she had been broadsided on a foggy night at a gravel intersection, which in combination with mounting financial problems on the farm that had led to his father's depression, alcoholism, and eventual suicide by hanging, came back to him.

"A mix," he answered.

Sensing she had crossed over the line, Kelly came back with, "What was your best moment?"

"Probably the forty-six-inch muskie I caught on the upper Apple."

"The best moment of your whole life is catching a fish? That's pretty sad!" The words were barely out of her mouth when she realized how harsh they were.

"It was a great fish," Jimmy said as he signaled the waitress for another beer, disappointed they weren't back at the station yet. "How about you?" he asked reflexively, not at all interested in the answer.

"1991, game six of the World Series, bottom of the eleventh, game tied three to three. I'm in the left field bleachers with some guy I thought I was in love with. Kirby Puckett cranks the game-winning home run. It goes right over our heads and lands about ten rows behind us.

"The place went crazy. We were hugging and high-fiving everybody. I really thought he was the guy I was gonna spend the rest of my life with and here we were together for this incredible moment."

"Where is he now?"

"I caught him two-timing me, so I dumped him. He got married, had two kids, and got divorced. He called me after they split up to see if I wanted to get back together. I told him to get..."

"Lost," Jimmy finished her sentence.

"Something like that; anyway, he's living with some teenage high school dropout now. Total loser!"

"But at the time it was good."

"The best. Any of your good moments involve a female?" Kelly asked.

"Just the ones with Maggie, my lab."

"Hmmm, farm boy whose only intimate relationships are with animals. We probably don't need to go there."

Ignoring her, he added, "senior prom was okay, and I've had girlfriends that were all right. We had some good times, but you gotta understand, it's a comparison thing. When a big ass muskie slams the plug, there's just nothing like it. They rip line off the reel till you can smell the gears smokin'. They make these great runs and then explode out of the water. Sometimes you get 'em in; sometimes you don't, but it's always a gas."

"My guess is you're gonna be slammin' your own plug for a while. Any good moments that don't involve fish?" she asked, losing interest, and signaling the waitress for another chardonnay.

"Frank thought I needed a break from the farm and offered to hire help for part of a summer, so a buddy and I took my truck up the Al-Can Highway to Alaska. Beat the shit out of it - had to replace a cracked windshield and give her a new paint job when we got back. Anyway, we spent most of that summer bummin' around Alaska.

"The whole trip was great but the best was when we were up at McKinley over the solstice, Denali to be politically correct. It was so cool that it never got dark. We'd spent the day hiking some pretty wild terrain. Went through these beautiful alpine meadows full of flowers, saw grizzlies, and waded a couple glacial melt streams that were like chocolate milk and so fast that even knee-deep water could knock you over. So it's about midnight, and the sun was stuck just above the horizon - seemed like it just stood still."

Kelly noticed that Jimmy's mind was no longer in the train.

"We were sittin' on this bluff overlooking a pretty incredible valley with about a two-thousand-foot cliff ten feet away from us. We're sittin' there reading from a book of Robert Service poems - mostly his macho Yukon stuff, although we were reading 'The Joy of Being Poor' at the time. Sounds pretty dorky, but all of a sudden, this golden eagle rides an updraft from below us and stops just beyond the edge of the cliff, maybe another ten feet out, eye level with us and stays there for five or six seconds. You could see the updraft blowing through its outer feathers, and we just stared at each other. We hadn't seen the mountain all day because of clouds, and about a half hour before this the clouds had broken up. So straight behind the eagle, who's eye to eye with us, is the tallest mountain in North America. Then the eagle cups his wings just a bit – catches all the air, and a minute later he's a thousand feet above us. I suppose that, like the DNA thing, the majesty of that eagle can be categorically reduced to its taxonomic, anatomic, and functional components: phylum, order, family, bone, muscle, feather, and its use of Bernoulian aerodynamics, but I think you lose something in the process." Taking a big swallow of his MGD, he added, "It was just a moment, but it was pretty cool."

"Let me guess. *Dead Poets Society* is your favorite movie," Kelly said.

"*Carpe diem.*"

"*Carpe momento.*"

"*Touché.*"

Staring out into the varied shades of darkness and shadows, Kelly was reminded of a mountain experience of her own. Backpacking and fly-fishing in Montana's Beartooth Wilderness for a week with friends, she had then spent a second week by herself after her friends had packed out. Her last night had been at Mirror Lake, which was nestled within a jagged basin. She had the entire place to herself and the evening rise of rainbow trout on the lake had produced good action on her #18 Adams fly. The remainder of that evening had been recorded later, by candlelight in her tent, pitched on a grassy knoll by the lake:

> "I reeled in my fly for the last time on this trip to the mountains and began the walk back to camp with the opal moon already visible to the east. After putting away my fishing gear, I gathered a pile of wood, started a fire, and prepared a dinner of baked trout, asparagus soup and tea. Facing southwest as I eat, I gaze at a rainbow, which coincidentally seems to end near the Rainbow Lakes plateau. The colors are vivid and distinct; not blended together in the usual pastel, but each trying to outshine the other. To the south, a planet is now visible. The sun has set, but its rays add a rose-orange hue to the clouds to the north.

> The small fire is burning well, I have plenty of firewood and a hot tea. A golden eagle floats across the southern part of the basin and over the eastern ridge. It is very peaceful, and the mountains seem to be making amends for the ornery weather in mid-afternoon. I am comfortable. Nights have been the toughest part of being alone in the mountains.

> Loneliness cannot be denied, and fear is evoked by the slightest of movements/shadows/noises. But tonight, I don't mind being alone. I enjoy the comradery of being with others around the campfire at night; recalling the day's

events, discussing the relation (or disconnect) between the time spent in the mountains and the time spent out of them and the continuous cooking and eating. But tonight, my last night, I am grateful to be alone. I again look to the east and the moon is no longer visible behind an advancing billowy black wave of clouds.

They won't be here for a few minutes, so I pack things up for the night, rewarm my tea and stand in the twilight by the fire, watching them advance. The air is charged, and I can feel the hairs on my neck raising up. A cooling breeze and a few sprinkles strike my face. The clouds are in a dynamic state, continually changing shape and form; black nebulous clouds, intermixed with white cottony ones; the sun still making its fading presence known through reflected rays. As the wave of clouds reaches the perimeter of the basin, it splits, half moving along the south wall of the basin and half to the north. In the center of the split, the moon is again visible and bright. The clouds move along the basin perimeter and reunite behind me, clear starry sky above with three hundred degrees of storm clouds and flashing bolts of lightning around me, the only clear horizon being that containing the moon. The thunder becomes palpable, and the hair of neck and scalp are pulled by their roots. Then, quickly as it had come, the entire storm has passed, the sun is now completely gone, and I'm left with a brilliant summer nighttime sky. I stand there for another half hour as the fire reduces itself to embers, thoughts flowing like a mountain stream. Full of wonder, I follow the moon's light to my tent, grateful to have 'come home to a place I'd never been before.'

There wasn't much for conversation, so Kelly's mind stayed in the mountains, recalling her introduction to them as a teenager. Her family had gone west with a pop-up camper on a three-week national park tour. The first day at Rocky Mountain National Park they had done a short hike on a wood chip trail around Sprague Lake. She remembered that the lake was nice but most of her attention had been directed toward the signage for trails heading further up into the mountains.

The following morning, her mother had put some snacks and water into a small backpack, and Kelly headed out before sunrise with her younger brother to do some exploring. They passed Sprague Lake and kept going, no map, just taking whichever trail seemed to be leading them higher. The trees were getting smaller and fewer, with aspen being replaced by fir and spruce. They came upon a long snowslide that fed a small lake which fed this incredible crystal clear stream cutting through a meadow laden with alpine flowers, almost too beautiful to fully comprehend. The next thing they knew, they were above tree line altogether on the continental divide, this magical highway extending from Mexico to Canada. She wanted to just keep going, not sure whether to go north, or south, but just wasn't ready to leave this place so they lingered on the cornice of Taylor Peak; not having watches, but realizing from the sun's descent that they needed to start down. The day was slipping away from them.

They slid down part of the snowslide, walked along the shoreline of the lake beneath it, and followed that creek through the meadow, then back on a trail, with increasing number and size of trees as then went. The sun had dropped out of sight and darkness was setting in as they reached the campground to find that their mother had alerted the park rangers of her lost children. She had initially been pretty upset, but their father was more interested in hearing about what they had seen, what they had done.

Kelly then thought of her next time in the mountains, while in high school; a Young Life trip to Frontier Ranch near the Collegiate Range. She had climbed Mount Chapman, helping a younger girl with cerebral palsy get to the summit. She had never been quite the same after that day, after that week.

They both noticed the lights of the train station. Kelly couldn't resist, "So how does tonight rate on your scale of moments?"

"All right," Jimmy answered.

"Just all right?"

"Well, the food was good, the beer was cold, and the company was better than the last couple of blind dates Frank set up for me."

"Blind dates? What are you talking about?"

"You don't really think he and Alice needed a nurse tonight? We go out to eat all the time and manage okay. He's trying to set us up."

"He's paying me $20 an hour plus dinner to go out with you? That's just great! I'm surprised he didn't offer me another $50 to get you laid!"

"Frank has more respect for you than that. I bet he would have gone $100."

"You know, for a while there you had me goin'. I actually thought you were a nice guy like Frank, and interesting too, but I was wrong and am probably wrong about Frank. You're both pigs!" she screamed, standing up with increasing decibels. "Gee, I wonder why you have such a tough time keeping a girlfriend and the only teats you get your hands on are in the cow barn. I'm out of here! Tell Frank he can keep his stinkin' money!"

Jimmy watched her go down the aisle toward the stairs and looked at the three closest tables where the couples were all looking at him. He mouthed the letters, *"PMS."* Two of the husbands immediately nodded sympathetically. The third looked first at his wife, caught her glare, and didn't look back.

Kelly went to the lower level, intending to tell Frank off, but saw him and Alice hand in hand, eye to eye, and chose not to barge in. She didn't know if Jimmy could get them back to Willow Manor, but he'd have to find a way because she wasn't going to be a part of this anymore.

When Jimmy came to the table without Kelly, Frank asked where she was.

"She had to go."

"Pissed off another one, huh? What happened this time?"

"Ah, you know how they are, Frank. Ya say one wrong thing, and they overreact. Next thing ya know...." Jimmy caught Alice's look and left it at that.

He helped Alice down the aisle and off the train to a bench outside the station before coming back for Frank. After calling for the nursing home van to come pick them up, Jimmy browsed through the small station gallery of old black-and-white photos from the lumbering days while Frank and Alice sat close together on the bench in the cooling summer night air and talked of the glory days of passenger trains.

The photos took Jimmy's imagination back a century to a time he thought he would have enjoyed - a lot of hard work, but a simpler time to have lived.

Chapter Ten

Although Tony Mihalik was a pain to have at home, it was more painful for his wife to be alone, so she arranged for them to move into an assisted living facility where they could live independently, but with help for Tony and help with meals and transportation. For a moving-out gift, Frank gave Tony - actually his wife - a box of nasal strips.

Frank's new roommate was Richard Carlson. Richard had been born in Devils Lake, North Dakota. When he was nine, he had a transient episode of right-sided body weakness which resolved. Two weeks later he developed flu-like symptoms, and the weakness returned. He remembered falling while reaching for a comic book on his bedroom shelf at home. One week later he was at Sister Kenny Institute in Minneapolis being treated for polio. He remembered Elizabeth Kenny, an RN from Australia, as "a large, imposing woman built more like a linebacker, with white hair and a rough demeanor, but very gentle. She moved through the place like a whirlwind - always on the run."

Richard had been at Sister Kenny most of July, August, and September of 1947. At one point, there were a hundred and twenty five kids aged five to twelve in one large room. "At first they didn't even know what polio was - whether it was a virus or not. Everyone got quarantined for two weeks and got massive doses of penicillin." The main treatment was hot packs and range-of-motion exercises. "They also tried a lot of experimental stuff."

Richard often went to the gym alone with a therapist to do active exercise. They did calisthenics and played ball games. He thought this helped him more than the passive treatment program did. There was "a certain type of fraternity" among the kids.

He remembered Dale Nutter from Texas, another 9-year-old with a lanky build, crew cut, red hair, and freckles. His dad was an oil millionaire and would come up frequently, bringing the kids candy and comic books. He remembered Bobby Wise, a kid from Centralia, Illinois, who became the poster child for Sister Kenny, and he remembered a kid from Winsted, Minnesota, who was paralyzed from the neck down and eventually died.

Due to overcrowding, there was one adult put on the kids' ward. Vic Riddle was a photographer from "down around Red Wing" who taught the kids how to take pictures and develop film. He met Rosalyn Russell, who played Sister Kenny in the movie *Sister Kenny*, when she was at the institute doing a promo for the film. Richard remembered her as being "slender and attractive, very different from the real Sister Kenny."

"At any given moment in our lives we feel so advanced. Back then the atomic bomb was a big deal. It was during the cold war, and they used to tell us kids if we didn't quiet down at night, the Russians would come and drop the bomb on us. Now we don't know how we could ever get by without cell-phones - just a different time and place."

Richard's polio left him with significant residual right-sided weakness, a right leg that was two-and-a-half inches shorter than his left and essentially no abdominal wall musculature. Despite his best attempts at weight control and weightlifting, he had the habitus of a swollen wood tick with a massively distended abdomen, unrestrained by an abdominal wall that consisted of little more than a thin sheet of connective tissue with overlying fat and skin. His thickly jowled face was topped with thinning reddish-brown hair, partially hanging over his matte silver Aviator-style glasses. Richard had been living independently with a job in marketing for an office products company.

He had been having frequent bladder infections and had complained to his doctor of passing gas with his urine. A colon X-ray had shown an inflammatory condition of his colon that caused it to communicate with his bladder. The involved portion of colon had been removed, and the bladder repaired.

He had made it through the operation all right, but the surgery had set his ongoing physical therapy program back . He wasn't strong enough to go straight home from the hospital and needed some time at Willow Manor as a transition.

Richard was a lot more demanding roommate than Tony had been, and didn't exactly endear himself to the nurses. Comments like, "You seem like a pretty good nurse, but your perfume makes me want to barf," didn't help. The nursing and physical therapy staff worked extra hard to get Richard back to baseline as quickly as possible so he could return home.

Frank initially had a similar reaction to Richard, but as he got to know him, he found him to be interesting and engaging - much more so than Tony had been. Jimmy spent a fair bit of time talking with Richard while Frank was sleeping or at therapy and found him to have a very organized perspective, someone for whom a handicap had involuntarily created the same type of social isolation and thought process that Thoreau had sought voluntarily.

Chapter Eleven

In the weeks that followed, Jimmy thought about Kelly and Kelly thought about Jimmy. She more frequently scanned the hallway to Frank's room and often glanced in as she walked by to see if he had any visitors. Jimmy increased his visits to Frank from nearly every day to twice or even three times a day, becoming more aware of what shifts Kelly was working and surveying the hallways more thoroughly than he had previously.

When Kelly was Frank's nurse, Jimmy was cool but attentive as she checked Frank's vitals, did a brief neurological exam, checked for bed sores, and asked a battery of questions about pain, weakness, dizziness, appetite, bowel activity, etc. Frank would pull Jimmy into the discussions as it moved into non-medical topics and would occasionally feign sleep to take himself out of the discussion altogether. The other nurses knew about the night on the dinner train and monitored the awkward courtship.

One Friday afternoon, Tina, another nurse who was a decade older than Jimmy and double her ideal body weight, mentioned to him that after the evening shift several of the nurses were heading downtown to Cat Ballou's for a drink and to catch a local band. She slipped in that Kelly was planning to go and Jimmy was welcome to join them. They got off at eleven o'clock and were going straight down.

Jimmy thanked her, but said he had to get up early the next day and probably wouldn't make it.

Jimmy was halfway through his first pint of St. Croix Maple Ale when the seven nurses came through the back door at Cat Ballou's. He was sitting at the bar listening to a local four-guy band that was surprisingly good for the size of the bar they were playing in. The place was long, narrow, and dark with a makeshift elevated stage near the back entrance where the nurses had come in. Although there weren't a lot of smokers the ventilation system didn't do much to get rid of the smoke that was generated, and it hung near the ceiling in slow-moving swirls, most apparent near the dim recessed lights.

The twenty by fifteen foot linoleum dance floor was empty but for three women dancing near the center. There was a life-sized Victorian style painting of a nude, full-figured blonde on the wall between the bar and the stage that caught Jimmy's eye and impressed him with the attention to detail.

Tina, the overweight nurse that had invited Jimmy, noticed him and came up to the bar, asking Jimmy how long he'd been there and inviting him to join them at their table near the stage and across the bar. She made reference to the oil painting and mentioned how embarrassing it had been to pose for it. Jimmy withheld comment as he grabbed his remaining beer in a pint-sized mason jar and got up to follow Tina to the nurse's table.

The table was too near the speakers to allow for much in the way of conversation while the band was playing. "Pink Cadillac" gave way to a respectable version of "Brown Sugar" prompting Tina to grab Jimmy's left arm and pull him toward the dance floor, snarling "all right, farm boy, let's see what you got."

Tina had left Jimmy no choice but to be dragged onto the linoleum with his dance partner shifting into high gear on arrival. Jimmy reluctantly and stiffly shuffled along with her, wishing that he were somewhere else.

Then a husky fellow with thin blonde hair and gold wire-rimmed glasses wearing a rust-and-brown serape came up from the audience to sing "La Bamba." Jimmy was impressed by the seemingly perfect enunciation of the Spanish lyrics and felt the "*espaniol*" that lies dormant in every male of Anglo descent come to surface. If Jimmy ventured away from domestic beers, it was usually to a Tecate, Dos Equis or Carte Blanc with a lime. He had stayed away from Corona because he had heard somewhere that somebody had tested a bottle of it and found traces of human urine. Although he doubted the story, he just couldn't bring himself to drink one. The only mixed drink he ever ordered was a margarita - rocks with salt, avoiding the fruit-flavored ones unless they had mango. He routinely put enough Tabasco on his morning eggs to draw beads of sweat to his forehead.

Jimmy had never traveled south of Iowa, but often pictured himself, the only gringo in town, washing down his *huevos* and *frijoles* with a can of cold Tecate on the shaded patio of a dusty cantina in a remote village somewhere in the Chiapas; a hot, dry morning with the smells of frying peppers, onions, and tortillas mixing with the sounds of a Spanish guitar; all wafting from the adobe kitchen. He had spent too much time trying to figure out how Butch and Sundance could have escaped on that fateful day in Bolivia when they had burst out into the bright sunlight of the courtyard - guns blazing, a moment captured in the poster on the wall of the milking parlor opposite the poster from Metallica's '91 US tour. Recently, he had found himself contrasting the balls-out departure of Butch and Sundance with the bit-by-bit departure of Frank, coming to no real judgments or conclusions - just thinking about it a lot.

Toward the end of the song, he loosened up and displayed a smoothness that impressed the table of nurses who had been watching with amusement. When the Zebra Mussels covered the Romantics' "That's What I Like About You," the nurses saw dance steps that had only been seen by the parlor girls in black and white back at the farm.

Jimmy and Tina created plenty of room for themselves on the now-crowded dance floor until Tina made eye contact with Kelly and motioned her to come out, initially getting a shake of her head as a response. With Tina's persistence, Kelly got up and wormed her way among the other dancers to send Tina back to the table with a friendly elbow to the ribs.

Jimmy and Kelly finished out the song after which the band promptly announced they were going on break and would be back in a few minutes.

"Pretty good band. You come down here often?" Jimmy asked as he started moving back toward their table.

"Maybe once a month."

"Ah, can I get you something to drink?"

"Thanks, but we have a tab going, and it looks like they ordered me another vodka grapefruit," she said, sitting back down at the crowded table.

"You two looked pretty good out there," one of the other nurses observed as Jimmy sat down and took a gulp of his beer, which had warmed considerably.

"For half a song," Kelly responded, looking over at the band's table beneath the nude blonde where they had settled in with a group of friends and seemed in no hurry to get back up on the stage.

Jimmy did have to get up early the next morning and, after glancing at his watch, told the group that he had to get going. Tina tried to get him to stay, but not even "the hen house needs a rooster" changed his mind.

Kelly said nothing as Jimmy got up, but then got up herself and more privately thanked him for coming, saying, "I'll probably see you back at Willow."

Jimmy had started to turn toward the door but turned back to face Kelly and asked, "You doing anything tomorrow afternoon?"

"Why?" she asked with an anticipatory chill at the back of her neck.

"Oh, I'm just going fishing out on the river and wondered if you might want to come along." Then backtracking, he added, "I know you're not that big on fishing, and you probably have to work or have other stuff to do. I didn't mean it as a date or anything, just fishin'."

"I actually have the weekend off and don't have any other plans. Sure, I'll go."

"Okay, great. Well, how about if I pick you up around noon?"

"Sounds good," she said, scribbling her address and phone number on a bar napkin. "What should I bring?"

"Not much, I'll have all the fishing stuff and will pack up a cooler. It may get a little chilly out on the river, especially toward dark, so you probably should bring some warm clothes. Otherwise I should have everything."

Then he asked, "Do you have a fishing license?"

"No, but I can get one in the morning. St. Croix River?"

"Yep."

"So a Minnesota license will do?" Kelly asked.

"Sure will."

"Great."

"Okay, well, I'll see you tomorrow at noon."

"See you then," she said, turning back toward the table.

"What was that all about?" Tina pried. "Sounds like you got a hot date with the farm boy."

"Hardly, we're just goin' fishing tomorrow."

"Fishing?" one of the other nurses inquired with more than a touch of disdain, "quite the Romeo."

Chapter Twelve

Earlier that evening, on the front porch at Willow Manor, Frank had asked Jack what got him into nursing.

"Back in high school I was on a Russian literature kick for a while, just couldn't get enough of it. I tried to pattern myself after Dostoyevsky's Alyosha Karamazov, but soon realized it just wasn't in me. Anyway, I read this short story by Tolstoy about a successful lawyer named Ivan who was dying. The story was mainly about the superficiality of his life, his cold and detached relationships with clients and family, what he thought was important. I can't remember what he was dying from, but the doctors treated him with detachment and without a personal connection, really doing very little to help him.

"Ivan had a servant named Gerasim who spent time with him, elevated his legs, kept him clean, tried to comfort him - basic nursing stuff. Gerasim helped him deal with his dying more than anything the doctor did. I guess the seed for becoming a nurse was planted. Forgot about Gerasim, and Tolstoy, for quite a few years."

"So after high school, I took some general and computer courses at the community college, tended bar, and played a lot of softball."

"Softball, huh? You don't look like much of a slugger," Frank commented, referring to Jack's slight build and crippled left arm.

"Well, I wasn't exactly Ken Griffey, Jr., but I was a hell of a pitcher. Good fielder too. Tucked my glove under my left arm while I pitched. Had plenty of time to put it on while the ball was in the air. After snagging a comebacker, I'd just pop it in the air, shake off my glove, grab the ball, and throw. Nothing to it."

"How about hitting?"

"Led our team in batting every year. I was pretty quick so I could usually out-run anything on the ground to the left side; and if they played up on me, I'd just pop it over their heads. Most of the guys just see how far they can hit it and end up being a long out."

"Must have been quite a show."

"Nothing like our base coaches were. Our team was sponsored by a strip club, The Happy Warrior. For out-of-town tournaments, we'd have strippers for base coaches. Every time we rounded first or third, their shirts went up. We were Class B ball, but got big crowds. I'm sure it violated city ordinances, but they never stopped us, and it wasn't because they didn't know about it. We had the town cop and a couple of sheriffs at every game. They were always up against the fence by first and third, just to make sure there weren't any problems. We got invited to a lot of tournaments.

"Anyway, when I met Jenny in theater class, we started going out, and I realized I needed to get a bit more serious about school and jobs -- actually, she decided that. So I remembered Gerasim and applied to nursing school. We got married the summer I finished. Jenny had been teaching grade school for about a year already, and I got a job in a coronary care unit at a downtown hospital. Worked there a couple of years and liked it pretty well, but when Jenny got pregnant, we decided to move out of the city. We've been here six years now, and had a couple more kids, two girls and a boy. I'm sure that'll be it.'

"I'm thinking about applying to nurse anesthesia school or some kind of business program. If I get into either one, I'll still try to pick up some hours here while I'm going to school."

"Well, don't forget why you went into nursing in the first place."

"I won't. I'm just ready to try something different."

"You said your dad had pancreatic cancer. Are your parents still alive?"

"Mom is. Dad died shortly after we moved here. He lived long enough to see the ultrasound pictures of his first grandchild."

"That's too bad," Frank said.

"Yeah, it wasn't good."

"I suppose you've seen a few die around here."

"Quite a few."

"Do they suffer much at the end?"

"No, most just seem to die in their sleep. I can't remember any that really suffered much. You wondering about that for yourself?" Jack asked.

"Well, sort of. I worry most about not being able to get enough air to breathe; that's a terrible feeling."

"I know what you're talking about, but I think the body has a way of telling the brain not to worry about it. We have patients here with very low levels of oxygen in their blood that seem pretty comfortable right up to the end. They don't seem to be fighting for air. A little morphine or a fentanyl patch can help with that.

'The toughest ones are when the family gets divided on how aggressive to be. Often, it's the son or daughter that hasn't been involved with the care of an aging parent who show up near the end and feel guilty and want everything possible to be done - feeding tubes, IVs, hospitalizations, stuff like that. Or they don't want anything done and want care to be withdrawn because they see part of their inheritance paying the bills.

'The family that has been involved has watched the decline and is usually comfortable letting things take their natural course. The patients themselves have often slipped beyond being able to make those decisions for themselves. A living will can usually help avoid some of those decisions that can tear a family apart at a time when they should be coming together. Sometimes though, a dying family member can pull a family back together because it changes their perspective.

'Back when I was doing hospital nursing, I took care of a lady who was in her fifties. She was admitted with a nagging cough and shortness of breath with a chest x-ray that looked like pneumonia in both lungs. They checked her sputum for bacteria and didn't find much. After a couple days of IV antibiotics, she still had the cough, and the chest x-ray didn't look any better, so they got a CT scan and did a needle biopsy. That night her doctor came by to tell her that the biopsy had found cancer; and because it was on both sides, there probably wasn't going to be a lot that could be done. Her first question was whether she would live long enough to see her 14-year-old son graduate from high school to which she was told that she probably wouldn't."

Jack continued on, "After the doctor left, she told me that she and her husband had separated six months before and that her son lived with her. She had left her husband because she felt he was more committed to his job than to his family and had become detached and harsh. I asked her if she wanted me to call him and she very firmly said no. She must have changed her mind 'cause she called him around midnight herself. He showed up shortly after that and they talked until five or so in the morning. He later told the day nurse that after he left the hospital, he just drove around for three hours before showing up at work at eight o'clock, not having slept, shaved, or showered and wearing jeans and a T-shirt.

'He told his boss about his ex-wife and that they had decided it would be best for him to move back home so there would be some continuity for their son when his mother died. He also told his boss that he had realized shortly after his wife and son had moved out, that she was right - he had become a jerk. He had hoped more than anything for another chance, but that this wasn't how he wanted it to be - he wished he could trade places with her.

'His boss told him to take as much time off as he needed with full pay - that his job would be there when he got back. He was a little surprised and even disappointed that they could get by without him, but by ten o'clock he was back at the hospital to pick up his wife who was being discharged. I never heard any more about how things went or how long she lived."

"How did it go when your dad died?" Frank asked.

"It was really sad, but one pretty remarkable thing happened. Dad's greatest passion was watching us kids play ball. My two younger brothers were better than I was, but we all played a lot of baseball growing up. Anyway, a local softball team I played with was gonna be in a weekend tournament in my parent's town, so I got my brothers to play for us. Dad came out to watch us the first day. He had watched us in hundreds of games, in different sports, from Little League through college, but it was the first time we had all played on the same team.'

"He was pretty weak and thin, but I can still see him hanging over the fence by our team's bench. I was pitching, one brother was at short and the other at first. It was the bottom of the seventh - and last - inning. We were ahead by one run and the other team had runners on first and third with one out. The batter hit a one hopper back to me. I flipped it to my brother at short as he crossed second and then he threw it to my other brother at first for a double-play to end the game. Turned out to be the last game and the last play he saw.'

"Afterward, we went to Dad's favorite restaurant. He didn't eat much, but it was the first time he seemed really at peace with what was happening, and we all had a pretty good time. He didn't have the strength to watch us play the next day; in fact, that was the last time he left the house before he died."

"I think you chose the right profession, Jack, but this seems like a tough place to work."

"It's not the most glamorous... but... sometimes late at night I sort of think of Willow Manor as a coral reef in the Caribbean..."

"You've got quite an imagination..." Frank said.

"...back in the 1800s and the patients that get admitted here are Spanish galleons crashing on the reef in fierce tropical storms," Jack continued.

"You're losing me, Jack."

"The ships themselves are broken and twisted and will never sail again, but they carry with them a rich treasure in history and knowledge that may or may not ever be retrieved. Ivan Robansky, down in 142, was a Russian nuclear physicist back in World War II, but the only stories he ever tells are about catching pollywogs as a kid back in his native Russia, a story he tells all day... every day. I don't think we'll ever know much about the treasure he carries with him, much less retrieve it."

Jack looked at Frank, looked at the setting sun, and said, "We'd better get you back to your room." He got no argument from Frank, and they headed back in.

Chapter Thirteen

J immy pulled into the access area, which consisted of a small, grav-
eled clearing on a wooded bend in the river. Six-foot-high retain-
ing walls of creosote-stained railroad ties held back the bank along
the concrete slope to the river. He deftly backed the boat trailer down
until the back tires were half under water. Emergency brakes set, Jimmy and Kelly both hopped out, and Jimmy unlatched and winched
the boat into the water.

A firm current gently pushed the boat downstream as Jimmy
guided it off the trailer and up against the shore. Kelly held the bow,
while Jimmy pulled the trailer up to the empty parking lot. The
downstream portion of the clearing had a grassy strip with a picnic
table between the gravel and the woods. Most of their tackle and gear
was already in the boat, so Jimmy just had to grab the cooler out of the
pickup bed before walking down to the boat.

It was a showcase autumn day with the yellows and reds of the birches and maples mixed with varied greens of the pine and spruce, accented by the striking white bark of the paper birches, all mirrored off the clear flat water. The sun's rays were undiminished by the occasional clump of cottony cumulus clouds, giving an uncommon warmth for early October, but with a crispness in the air that smelled of fall. There wouldn't be many of these days left, and on such a day boating any fish was far second to just being out.

Maggie was already in the boat, tail banging against the fiberglass as Jimmy helped Kelly in and pushed out as he hopped in himself. The boat drifted noiselessly as Jimmy moved to the back and started the sixty-horse engine. He started off quarter throttle down river as he pointed out a spot, just downstream from the access, where they'd often dive in off the high bank. The pool just below the bank was at least fifteen feet deep and clear enough to see if there were any downed trees or branches to avoid.

Picking up to half throttle, Jimmy flipped around his Daiawa cap to keep it from blowing off and pointed toward a motionless great blue heron perched on a graying snag just above the water along the near bank.

Just as Kelly picked out the bird from the branches, it leaned forward, raised its great wings, and launched itself down river, paralleling the boat's course until it had enough elevation to bank over the shoreline trees and circle back upstream to another fishing spot.

Although Jimmy had seen hundreds of them, he was never

unimpressed by the size and grace of these beautiful birds. Kelly, on the other hand, had never seen one so close and was wide-eyed, while Maggie, having staked out her front most position, broke her nose-into-the-wind pose to follow the flight of the bird.

"Great blue heron," Jimmy said quietly.

"Wow, they're huge!"

"Yeah, they sure are," he said, enjoying her enthusiasm. He hadn't known how taking Kelly fishing would go, but it seemed to be off to a good start.

Jimmy pointed out hooded mergansers and redheads and a small flock of mallards tucked against a wooded bank. A large flock of noisy Canadian geese flew overhead, not yet conveying the sense of urgency they would have in a couple weeks. They watched an osprey miss a couple of attempts at suckers in swift shallow ripples near the far bank and saw two bald eagles, one adult perched on an oak stump overlooking a quiet pool, and a still brown-headed juvenile gliding across the river ahead of them, just above tree top height.

Kelly's thick Dartmouth sweatshirt, given to her by an older brother who went there, was plenty to keep her warm as Jimmy sped to full throttle with the widening of the river. Her family had done a lot of lake boating and water skiing, but she enjoyed the anticipation of new vistas around each bend of the river. This ended as the river widened to the point of essentially becoming a small lake. Jimmy guided the boat toward a narrow, wooded point jutting out into the river-lake, and Kelly figured that was the fishing spot. The boat slowed on its approach and Jimmy cut the engine as the anchor was dropped.

Kelly had counted six fishing rods on a rack that were fully rigged. "This is a good muskie spot," Jimmy said as he lifted off a stout bait casting rig with a foot-long, buck-tailed lure. "Want to give it a try?"

"No, I brought a book. I'll just watch you and maybe try it later," she said as she pulled a bottle of chardonnay out of the cooler and filled half of a sixteen-ounce plastic cup.

Jimmy was anxious to get at it himself and didn't mind Kelly's deferral. Kelly watched for a while, impressed with how far he could launch the oversized lure, but then settled into her novel - and the wine.

Half an hour and very little conversation later, Jimmy asked Kelly if she had seen the follow.

"Did I see the what?"

"The follow, big fella followed the bucktail right up to the boat."

"Oh, well, maybe next time he'll bite it," more interested in her book than the muskie.

The peaceful afternoon was interrupted as half a dozen squawking crows flew overhead in pursuit of a red-tailed hawk. They both looked up to watch the crows dive-bomb the hawk as it made its way to the opposite shore.

"Why do they do that?" Kelly asked.

"I don't know. Hawks aren't really much of a threat to crows. I think it's more of an attitude thing. Hawks are sort of aloof and act superior to crows. I think the crows, which are smart birds, don't like it, so they try to make life miserable for the hawks."

"Do they ever hurt the hawks?"

"The hawk is in no danger of its life from devils black; just feathers and a bit of pride he'll lose in this attack."

"I walked into that one. Who wrote that?"

"I did."

"Sounds like there might be more to it."

"In October of '83, I was in my truck on the way here to fish at about five in the morning, listening to the radio, and they broke in with a news flash about a terrorist bombing of a U.S. embassy in Beirut. A bunch of U.S. guys got killed. Didn't think too much about it until I was out here fishing and saw what we just saw. Seemed like they were kind of similar."

"Tell me the whole thing."

"Naw, it's kind of long and some of the rhyme is a bit forced."

"I don't care. I'm not going anywhere," she said, refilling her glass with wine.

"All right.

"The morning fog's a blanket over water flat as glass.

The St. Croix at this time of day has beauty unsurpassed.

No one else is at this place, the river is my own.

Last night's events are tough to grasp. It's nice to be alone.

Thoreau, he wrote of many things, of wonders oft neglected.

Of dividends from nature's gifts going uncollected.

Of moonlit ponds, Katahdin's peak, of quiet desperation.

I doubt that he would want to join the current generation.

Service wrote of frigid cold, of huskies on the trail.

Of bannock baking in the coals, of hobos on the rail.

A race of men that don't fit in, a race that can't stay still.

A race not meshed in stocks and bonds, not harnessed to the till.

Dear Abbey writes of canyon rims, of eagles on the air,

Of stark but wondrous features of the desert solitaire.

Disdain he shows towards those who mold a landscape blessed to all.

Towards those whose enterprise it is to spread the urban sprawl.

I was just a child when Martin told us of his dream.

I've seen the speech in black and white, with black and white the theme.

A dream wherein the people of all nations, races, creeds could get along.

A dream yet unfilled as global hatreds fester on.

These mentor's words perfuse my brain as I peruse the dawn.

The orange-red sun is rising now, the fog is nearly gone.

A red-tailed hawk comes into view, reflecting new daylight.

It glides among the limestone bluffs and pines along its flight.

The hawk is a self-centered bird, sans diplomatic skills.

A feathered version of the shark, efficient are its kills.

With eagles, owls, and falcons: the reclusive birds of prey

Their talons sharp with beaks that shred the weak that fall their

way.

Defiant and aloof, they are the bullies of the block.

Their arrogance and attitude well-known amongst the flock.

Their posture spurns a hatred from the fowl of other bays.

A hatred that may manifest in terrorist ways.

The tranquil tone of morn is broke as raucous crows fly o'er.

Advancing toward the red-tailed hawk a furlong out from shore.

The hawk is in no danger of its life from devils black.

Just feathers and a bit of pride he'll lose in this attack.

The crows will pester and harass then slip back from the race.

Until they feel it's time again to put the hawk in place.

But how the hawk would love to grasp a squawking neck of crow

And show those little bastards just how far this game can go.

The hawk will seldom catch the crow, the master of the game.

And even if he does, there's always more from whence it came.

The hawk has got to realize his attitude must cease.

Until he shows some empathy he will not know of peace.

The hawk and crows have flown away, their memory hangs on.

I'm saddened by last night's events, where does the blame belong?

Peace through strength the rational, our hawkish posture grows.

I wonder if we understand the ways of hawks and crows."

"Sounds like there was a dove among the hawk and crows that day," Kelly noted.

"Just seems like it wouldn't take much of a change in attitude on the hawk's part and all the birds could get along," Jimmy said.

"I don't think it would make any difference. I think the hawks and owls and eagles and whoever else is being harassed should just decide that enough is enough and join together and kick some crow ass. They could do a lot of damage and maybe stop the harassment altogether, without having to change who they are."

"I don't think they'd get all the crows, and the ones remaining will just be more pissed off and committed to making the hawk's life miserable. If the hawks had spent more time with the crows when they were younger, they might be a bit less arrogant toward them when they grow up," Jimmy speculated.

"I still think the hawk is the stronger bird and shouldn't be afraid to show it. If he shows a softer side, he'll just get taken advantage of...."

After a healthy swallow of chardonnay, she asked, "Know anything a little lighter?"

Without hesitating, he said, "*Little Miss Muffet sat on a tuffet eating her...*"

"Very funny," Kelly cut him off.

Reminding himself of a jingle he had written as part of a ninth-grade English assignment, Jimmy started again.

"Make that:

Little Miss Kelly laid on her belly, kicking the ground in despair.

Fall was the season, her breath was the reason

her boyfriend no longer was there.

He said that her breath had the foul smell of death,

which made her shudder and cry.

He said 'settle down, honey and get out your money

for Mint Mouth is what you should buy.

Mint Mouth will brighten what you used to frighten.

No reason to be so forlorn.

The guys will do flips at the taste of your lips.

It's almost like being reborn.

So Little Miss Kelly got up off her belly and

went off to take his advice.

The bad breath she fought with the Mint Mouth she bought,

but she still needed something for lice."

"The girl in that poem just happened to be named Kelly," she noted with more than a trace of skepticism.

"Just a coincidence I guess."

"Some coincidence. Well, I'm ready to go after a muskie if you have the patience to show me how to cast that thing."

"Ever use a bait casting reel?"

"I don't think so."

Jimmy didn't want to spoil the afternoon with a messy backlash, so he put his rod back on the rack and grabbed a closed-faced reel that he had rigged up with a large red-and-white spoon. Kelly hadn't told Jimmy about the fly-fishing and some northern Minnesota lake fishing she had done; knowing how to cast, but feigning inexperience. Jimmy obliged with patient hands-on instruction. She learned quickly and was soon casting roughly two-thirds of the distance Jimmy had been. He pointed to spots to cast and gave specific instructions regarding speed of retrieval and rod action as well as making a figure of eight by the boat with the lure to give a following muskie a final chance to strike.

Kelly's mind drifted back to fishing in northern Minnesota. She remembered being nine years old and waking up one morning in their cabin to find that her dad and two brothers had gotten up early and gone fishing without her. Most of her morning had been spent hanging around the dock scanning the lake for their boat, which finally came back in. The fishing had been good and a stringer of walleyes, with a couple of average-sized northern pike, was hoisted onto the dock and pictures were taken.

Kelly had tagged along to the screened-in shack with a concrete slab sink and hose where her brothers had cleaned the fish. She watched as the sharpened knife was positioned right behind the gills and the cut down to the spine made. The cut was then taken back along the spine to the tail and stopped with less than an inch to go so the fillet could be flipped over and skimmed off the skin. The rib bones would then carefully be cut out and the fillet washed and dropped into an ice cream pail. The Y bones on the northerns took a bit more work and there was a mimeographed sheet on the wall describing the technique, which her 12-year-old brother had referenced a few times, but which wasn't needed by her 15-year-old brother. They had opened a few stomachs to see what the fish had been eating and identified minnows and crawfish. One northern had an eight-inch perch in its stomach, which had surprised Kelly by looking so fresh and unscathed. They finished with plenty of fillets in the bucket for a couple of family fish fries.

After the excitement had died down, Kelly had gone back to their cabin and complained to her mother about not being awakened to go with.

"Well, your dad has a list of things he needs to do this afternoon, but maybe Tom can take you out fishing for a while."

Kelly remembered the look her 15-year-old brother had given their mother, but he agreed to take her out "after lunch and a nap."

Kelly idolized her oldest brother, Tom, but hadn't seen him much the past couple of years with his schedule filled with work, sports, school activities, and girls.

Kelly remembered watching him sleeping on the couch after lunch, waiting for him to wake up. She deliberately had been as noisy as possible with the fridge, cupboard doors and shuffling newspapers. Finally, Tom partially opened his eyes and saw her staring at him from about three feet away.

"Well, looks like you're ready to go fishing," he said, as he pulled himself off the couch.

Tom had let Kelly steer the sixteen-foot Lund fishing boat with fifteen-horse Evenrud across the lake once he got it going. He had directed her towards a weedy shoreline, which opened into a small channel through which they passed into a smaller lake, which Kelly had not been to before. The larger lake had been choppy from the afternoon wind, but the smaller lake was calm except for fine ripples pushed across the surface by the gentle summer breeze.

They had anchored just outside a bed of lily pads with their white-and-yellow flowers soaking in the afternoon sun. The first thing Tom did was rig up an eight-inch sucker minnow on a jumbo hook with an oversized white- and-red bobber and chucked it out well away from the boat - for northerns. He then set up a pan fish rig with a piece of night crawler six feet below a small orange-and-red bobber.

They had caught a bunch of small sunfish, perch and rock bass which had been let go before Kelly had noticed the big bobber was nowhere to be seen. It had been pulled and bobbed some by the sucker minnow, hooked just in front of his dorsal fin, but had not stayed down for more than a few moments. Tom picked up the rod, pulled back hard to set the hook and handed the pole to Kelly saying, "it's all yours; feels like a big one."

She had the fight of her life with the pike stripping line and the drag buzzing as she tried to reel. Twice Kelly had the fish near the boat with her brother leaning forward with the landing net only to have it dive under the boat and strip off more line. She had finally worn it out and had gotten it up to where her brother could net it.

"Eight-and-a-half pounds," Tom had declared after weighing it, "bigger than I've ever caught."

They had put the pike on a stringer and got the fish back into the water where Kelly watched it for a while.

"Want to do any more fishing?" Tom had asked.

She had told him that was enough for today.

They had sat in the boat munching on the snacks and drinking pop from the cooler their mom had packed for them. Tom hushed Kelly and pointed to a family of low-riding loons, which had come surprisingly close, considering the commotion. There were two babies already the size of mallard ducks, and one adult that hung close together, with another adult that was larger and darker about thirty feet away from the others. They would periodically dive under for what had seemed an eternity, during which Kelly and her brother would try to guess where they would surface. After coming up the adults would give short calls that Tom said were separation calls and they would regroup. They had seen the larger one bring up a six-inch perch sideways in its bill and watched it reposition the perch so it could be swallowed headfirst.

Kelly and Tom watched a saucer-sized painted turtle come to the surface and poke among the lily pads for anything edible before popping back down and swimming off.

The warm afternoon sun finally pushed them into the lake as they jumped out of the boat after donning their snorkeling gear. Kelly watched her northern from under water and brought up clams from the bottom, which were placed in the minnow bucket. Thoughts of the fish fry finally encouraged Kelly to tell her brother, "maybe it's time to go back to the cabin."

Her dad met them at the dock and went back to get the camera after Kelly hoisted up the northern when they were still thirty yards out. Pictures were taken and Kelly had carefully taken the pike off the stringer and let it go. The dark green-backed fish hesitated over the sandy bottom in the clear water next to the dock before beginning to slowly swim away. Then, with a couple of quick tail flicks, it was gone.

After a dinner of the best fish she could remember, Kelly dug out a pool at the water's edge with rocks blocking the exit, into which went the clams and a few minnows. The lake was still except for incoming waves from passing boats, which would partially cave in the sandy sides of the pool, until Kelly and a neighbor girl her age who was helping did reparation. The northern Minnesota sunset was everything it should be, which preceded Kelly's releasing the minnows, dropping the clams off the end of the dock, and scrambling up the beach and through the scattered birch and pine to the cabin, swatting mosquitos and getting scolded by an agitated red squirrel as she went. The last sounds of the night as she drifted off to sleep were those mournful, magical, mystical, maniacal loons.

But more than the loons, or the other abundant wildlife from moose to mosquitoes, the creatures that came to mind first when she thought of "up north" were the Tiger Swallowtail butterflies floating in the afternoon breeze, among the trees, between the cabin and the lake.

Chapter Fourteen

Kelly kept at the casting for twenty minutes or so, then mentioned that her arm was getting sore. Checking the sun which looked to give just another couple hours of light, Jimmy told her to take two more casts and then they would move to a different spot to try for walleyes.

As she was halfheartedly doing the figure eight on her last cast a four-foot-long, dark green shadow made a quick pass at the lure and disappeared. Startled by the size, she asked, "what was that?"

"A nice muskie; he would have given you quite a fight."

"It was huge! I can't believe there are fish that big in here."

Smiling, he said, "yeah, and there's some a lot bigger than that one. After a follow like that, some folks get the fever so bad it's all they can think about."

"Well, that was pretty neat, but I think I'll get over it. Let's go try your walleye spot. If we get any, we can eat 'em, right?" she asked, remembering the beer-battered walleye at the family cabin.

Jimmy wasn't much of a chef, but he did do a nice job with fish. "Sure, I'll cook 'em up," he told her.

He lifted the anchor, started the engine, and scooted up river another half mile, slowing as he watched the depth gauge, suddenly killing the engine, and drifting upstream before the current reversed their direction. Two other rods were rigged with quarter-ounce jigs, to which he added a wiggling leech to his and a fathead minnow to Kelly's.

"There's a long gravel bar here that we're gonna drift over. Just let the jig drop to the bottom; you can feel when it hits.

Then lift your rod tip every few seconds and let the jig bounce along."

Kelly had a strike almost immediately and landed an eighteen-inch chunky walleye. "That'll eat up real nice," Jimmy said, putting supper in the live well.

There was nothing further that drift or the next. They had about an hour of light left with half of that needed to get back to the access.

As they started their third drift Kelly started losing interest. "Know any poems that aren't so serious or insulting?"

Jimmy thought the afternoon had gone pretty well and didn't want it to finish like the fiasco on the train. "How about Tennyson?" he asked, letting his jig drop to the bottom.

"Try me."

"The rain had fallen, the poet arose.

He passed through the town and out of the street.

A light wind blew from the gates of the sun

and waves of shadows went over the wheat.

He sat himself down in a lonely place and chanted a melody loud

and sweet that made....

"There we go," he said, leaning over his rod and letting out line as the tip bent slowly toward the water. "Suck it in... that's it... bingo!" He pulled back hard against the resistance to set the hook as the fish stayed deep and used the current to its advantage.

Kelly watched him work the twenty-three-inch walleye to the surface a couple of times before it showed signs of tiring.

Oh well, she thought, a passion for fishing beats the passion for corporate tax law that her last boyfriend had, as she reached for the net to help bring it in.

"That's okay; I got it," Jimmy said reaching over, unhooking and releasing the fish without lifting it out of the water.

They watched the fish hesitate as it gathered its strength and then dove back into the depths of the river. Jimmy added a sixteen-incher to the live well at the end of the drift. "That should be plenty."

The sun was just above the horizon with the orange melting into the pale blue of the sky. Jimmy reached into his duffel and pulled out a frayed down jacket for Kelly, which she gladly accepted as the air had become noticeably cooler with the sun's imminent departure.

As the coat was being zipped, Jimmy directed her attention to an osprey flying near the shore. "See the fish it's carrying?"

"I'm glad he finally got one."

"But he may not get to eat it."

"Why?"

"Look over there; the eagle's coming after it."

They watched as the eagle caught up with the osprey, slowed by its heavy cargo, and forced it to drop its dinner. The eagle then followed the fish down and easily picked the stunned fish off the surface of the water before flying off to a dead branch of an old oak to eat its ill-gotten goods while the osprey swung around and flew back up river.

"I feel bad for the osprey," Kelly said.

"Well, that's the way it is, but he won't starve. There's a lot of fish in here."

"What other animals are around here? Any wolves or bears?"

"There's a lot of coyotes, but it's not very often that wolves come this far south. I see bears along here quite a bit, especially at dusk."

"You do?" she asked, not really liking the sound of that. "Where do you see 'em?"

"Sometimes along the shore or by the campground we just passed. I see a big old black bear down by the access every once in a while. He probably finds fish guts along the bank after folks cleaned fish and didn't clean up after themselves."

The sun fell below the horizon as they trailered the boat. Jimmy began cleaning the fish on the picnic table. The fillets from the eighteen-incher were lying on the quart-sized, zip-locked bag that they would be sealed in for placement in the cooler. Jimmy had one side of the sixteen-incher done and was flipping it over as a splash directed his attention back to the river. The splash was more than even the largest of bass would make and not as sharp as a beaver tail slap. Directing his gaze toward the river, he noticed expanding rings about twenty feet out from shore through which a head popped up - Kelly's head. He watched as she breast-stroked away from shore with a smooth strength she had developed through a decade of competitive swimming.

Setting down the knife and wiping his hands on his pants, Jimmy hurried to the edge of the bank where Kelly had dived in. "Aren't you freezing?"

Turning back, she said, "It's a little cool at first, but you get used to it. Come on in. It feels great!"

"Ah... no thanks. I'll wait till next summer."

"Wimp!" she taunted.

"I didn't think we'd be skinny dipping on our first date."

"What date? You asked me to go fishin'. Our first date will be when you take me to a nice restaurant and a play or concert afterward. Besides, this water's cold enough that you couldn't do what you'd like to, even if I did let you."

Her words rolled around in his head as Kelly turned and swam slowly away from shore, giving Jimmy a chance to modestly leave his clothes in a pile on the ground and dive in. Her words rang true as he hit the water and the icy shock sucked the air from his lungs and pulled his testicles up into his throat.

Kelly laughed as he screamed and flailed, gasping for air upon reaching the surface.

"Christ, it's freezing!"

"Wimp," she repeated.

Jimmy almost said something about the extra layer of fat that women had, but didn't. He kept his arms and legs moving and warmed up enough to enjoy the charge the cold water gave him as they swam near, but not too near each other in the very dim light of the fading sun and just rising orange October moon. Maggie soon joined them out of nowhere.

Jimmy had trouble taking his eyes off Kelly, her vibrant eyes that captured even the minimal light, her wet hair that was pushed back over slender shoulders moving forward and back as she treaded water in front of him. His eyes, unlike his thoughts, stayed above the water.

Kelly was very aware of Jimmy's attention, but was nonchalant and just occasionally glanced his direction, showing more attention to Maggie, but toying with the idea of teasing him with a few strokes of back crawl.

The chardonnay that had built her bravado also accelerated her cooling off and she could feel her arms stiffen a bit. Kelly had hardly noticed the current when she had first dived in, but now was having some trouble keeping it from pushing her downstream.

"I think I'm gonna go to shore," she said with just a trace of panic in her voice.

"You okay?"

"Yeah, just getting a little tired."

"And hypothermic."

"Maybe a little..."

Jimmy looked toward shore. "The bank is too steep right here, and you won't make it back to the ramp. Let the current take you and follow me. There's a branch sticking out over there that we can grab and pull ourselves up."

As Maggie swam close to Kelly, Jimmy instructed her to hold onto Maggie's tail. Jimmy swam a sidestroke so he could keep an eye on Kelly and Maggie as they made their way toward shore, letting the current take them to the branch. Once there, Kelly had some trouble holding on, so Jimmy grabbed her forearm, pulled her to the bank and helped her up the rather steep rocky shoreline to a soft grassy recess. Kelly was shivering and her teeth were chattering.

"Stay here. I'll go get your clothes and the down jacket."

Then turning toward Maggie, he said, "stay here with Kelly."

Maggie ignored him as something else caught her attention and her deep growl erupted into angry barks directed toward the parking lot.

"What is it?" Jimmy asked, and again in a stronger voice "Maggie, stay here." As she started moving in the direction she was barking, Jimmy grabbed her collar and made her sit. The barking stopped, but the deep-throated growl continued even after Jimmy started back toward the truck. He was freezing himself as he bustled through the brush until a basal snort stopped him.

In the twilight by the picnic table, he saw what had set Maggie off: the silhouette of a bear, paws up on the table. The bear apparently tired of just getting the skin and guts, was now enjoying a first-class walleye dinner.

"All right, big fella," he said as he worked his way around him. "Just keep eating. It's all yours."

The bear watched him, snorted again, and went back to the fish.

"What is it?" a weakening voice came from behind him.

"Nothing."

Jimmy got within thirty feet of the bruin before dancing his way across the gravel in bare feet to his truck. He started the engine, cranked up the heater and grabbed a flashlight from under the seat. He pulled an old blanket from a compartment in the boat before swinging back around the picnic table and the bear to the water's edge, where their clothes were scattered on the ground and a nearby bush. He found his own t-shirt, jeans, and tennis shoes, which he put on before gathering up most of Kelly's clothes, her shoes, and the down jacket. Then he picked his way back through the woods to the bank where Kelly and Maggie lay huddled, with Kelly telling Jimmy she was okay through chattering teeth.

Jimmy left her the clothes, jacket, and blanket, along with the flashlight as he went back to finish dressing himself with his only light being that from the rising moon. Looking over toward the picnic table, he no longer saw the silhouette and hoped that the bear had gotten enough to eat and had been bothered enough by the commotion to make its departure.

"Everything okay?" Jimmy asked the downstream darkness.

He heard no response, but did see that the flashlight was moving in his direction. He walked toward the light and came upon Kelly and Maggie. Kelly again assured him that she was okay although still shivering. He told Kelly about the bear that had been helping himself to their fish at the picnic table, but told her he thought the bear was gone. This was less than reassuring to Kelly as they worked their way through the brush back to the edge of the clearing. Jimmy shined the flashlight toward the picnic table and confirmed the bear was no longer there.

A chill went up Kelly's already cold spine. "Where is he?"

"I don't know."

Maggie, who had dutifully stayed with Kelly from the bank up to the clearing, now made a beeline for the picnic table and raced around the table and the parking lot, all jazzed up by the fresh bruin scent. Jimmy grabbed her by the collar, lifting her off the ground with coarse audible wheezing from the pressure on her throat. The three of them quickly made their way to the pickup truck where Maggie was hoisted into the back and Kelly was helped into the toasty warm cab.

Jimmy jogged back to the picnic table, found his fillet knife and sheath. He shoved the newspaper, the zip-locked bag and fish remains into the cooler and tossed it into the back of the boat. Jimmy hopped into the driver's side cab and slid the flashlight and fillet knife under the seat, wiping his hands on his pants. Kelly's shivering and chattering had improved considerably and, as they looked at each other, they burst out laughing.

"That was fun - not very smart - but fun," Kelly remarked as she turned the heater down a notch. "This thing really kicks it out."

"Gotta have a good heater and a good radio," he said, turning up the volume on Van Morrison's "Brown-Eyed Girl."

Jimmy pulled out of the parking lot and onto the smooth asphalt with a three-quarter moon in front of them. They were immediately passed by a squadron of motorcycles, lured to the road that afternoon by perhaps the last great biking weekend of the year. The last in line was a three-hundred-fifty-pound fellow on his Roadster, complete with black leather chaps giving way to black leather boots and with sunglasses beneath his yellow bandana - despite the sun's having been down for nearly an hour. He came up quickly from behind them and swung around Jimmy's truck, scooting back in front of Jimmy just seconds before an oncoming semi passed by in the opposite lane. The biker's mid-back length brown hair blew straight behind him, allowing the lettering on the back of his skin-tight black T-shirt to be easily seen in Jimmy's headlights:

"If You Can

Read This

The Bitch

Fell off."

"My guess is the bitch has her own bike", Kelly speculated. Before a mile had passed, they were both warm and singing along to the radio. Kelly had that "game six in the bleachers" feeling. Jimmy cracked his window a couple inches and turned the heater down another notch.

"No fish dinner tonight," Kelly lamented.

"Sure we can. We'll head down to Dick's Bar in Hudson. They've got pretty decent fish."

"Oh, I'm not dressed for that," she said, looking down at her sweats and dirty tennis shoes with no socks.

"If anything, you're overdressed."

They didn't talk much on the thirty mile drive to Hudson, mostly listening to the radio and singing along to the songs they knew, both comfortable with the frequent gaps in conversation.

Jimmy parked the truck and trailer at the lot by Hudson Park, and they walked uphill to the bar.

Kelly liked Dick's. The eating area was informal but nice, and the food was good. When they were done eating Jimmy gave the waitress his cash and check card, the only plastic he owned. Kelly was in the restroom when the waitress came back to tell him the card hadn't gone through. He reflexively scooted out the back door before Kelly came back and ran across Main Street to the SuperAmerica gas station and found the cash machine, popping in the same card that hadn't gone through at Dick's. The "insufficient funds" that showed on the screen could just as well have said "Loser," and he headed back to Dick's, wondering how he was going to pay for their meal.

As he approached the table, he saw Kelly signing a credit card slip. He told her she didn't have to pay for dinner, but she told him it was the least she could do after the episode at the river. Jimmy didn't push it any further and they went back to the bar area. Jimmy did have enough cash for a couple of twenty-ounce Lucky Dogs, a few games of pool and a dozen songs on the jukebox.

Jimmy drove Kelly back across the 94 bridge, up 95 on the Minnesota side and back to her apartment. Even though it hadn't been a real date, he knew that at least a good night kiss was his if he went for it, but he held back. The goodbye was a bit awkward as they reaffirmed that it had been a fun afternoon and night, both not really wanting it to end, but it did.

On the way home, Jimmy stopped at the Fina Gas Station and used the last of his change to buy a St. Paul Pioneer Press newspaper. When he got back to the farm, he rummaged the entertainment section to see if any good plays were coming to town. Nothing really caught his eye except Kid Jonny Lang coming to the Blues Saloon. Dinner at a nice restaurant in St. Paul followed by a night with the blues phenom seemed like it might be a good first real date.

Chapter Fifteen

Jack noticed Frank and a new resident playing cribbage at a table in the lobby as he passed by on his way to the med room. He listened in to their mostly one-way conversation as the new guy recalled details of his experience as a paratrooper with the 101st Airborne, where he too had been in on the Normandy invasion. His story was different from Frank's in that he had been dropped behind enemy lines instead of being brought to slaughter on a beach that "hadn't been properly prepared in advance for the landing" as Gene put it. The difficulty the paratroopers had faced was mainly due to high winds that scattered the troops and made regrouping difficult. The wind had also blown a few into wooded areas where they were left hanging from trees and were easy targets for the Germans.

He had come across on the USS Wakefield and had staged in Bastogne prior to the invasion. Gene had been shot on a later mission where, after securing Dusseldorf, five GIs had been hit by a sniper that was found to be a "granny on a porch with a sawed-off 25-caliber rifle under her shawl." She was quickly dispatched by Sergeant Rory Brown with a shot from his pistol to her temple.

Gene Gorman was at Willow for a couple weeks of rehab after a left hip replacement. Frank told Gene more than he had told Jack about that day at Normandy. He also told him about his former wife Betty, his stroke and the prostate cancer that was progressing despite treatment.

Gene told Frank these were the wonder years. "Ya wonder what the hell's gonna go wrong next."

Frank appreciated having a mentally alert peer with something in common to hang out with. Gene came back to visit Frank a few times after he had been discharged from Willow and was back with his wife at home.

––––––––––––

Over the next few weeks Jimmy and Kelly saw a lot of each other. The night in the city with dinner at the St. Paul Grill followed by catching Jonny Lang at the Blues Saloon went well. Kelly was spending more time out at the farm and would usually stop by after working nights to have breakfast with Jimmy and then crash on his couch for a few hours before heading back to St. Paul for her afternoon classes. They hadn't spent any nights together yet, but they both felt the relationship was heading in that direction.

On the way out to the barn before dawn on a mid-November morning Jimmy realized that Maggie had gone blind. She was usually several steps ahead as they walked from the farmhouse to the barn. This morning, with the first rays bouncing off the clouds along the eastern horizon, she trailed behind; and when he looked back, Jimmy saw her following, but with a deliberate, unsteady gate. He called her name softly and as she came to him, he raised her head in his hands and in the diluted glow of the yard light he could see a bluish glaze to her non-tracking eyes. Jimmy knew dogs could get cataracts and figured that, although pricey, surgery could be done just like in people. Twice during milking Maggie had gotten kicked after bumping into the hind legs of a Holstein in the stanchions. It was tough for Jimmy to watch her banging into walls and stumbling on the steps of the parlor. He cut his other chores short after milking and took Maggie up to the house. He made extra bacon and eggs for her while he ate his own breakfast and looked up the phone number for Dr. Carling's office. He glanced up to see if Maggie was enjoying her morning treat, but the eggs and bacon were still sitting in the bowl which he had placed a foot from her nose. This was a dog that had a field trial champion father and could track a running rooster pheasant in the driest of conditions.

Jimmy got up and put the food two inches from her nose - no response. It wasn't until he gently pushed her nose into it that she wolfed it down and got up on her feet to awkwardly rummage around looking for more. Jimmy wondered if her problem was more than just cataracts. His thoughts were interrupted by the banging of the screen door as Kelly arrived after working the night shift. She had a bag of grocery odds and ends in one arm and a cup of Tom Thumb coffee in the other hand.

"What's up?" Kelly asked in a generic way as she put the groceries on the counter.

"Maggie's blind, and I don't think she can smell either."

"What?"

"Yeah, on the way to the barn this morning, I noticed she couldn't see. Just now she couldn't smell bacon and eggs right in front of her face. I was just about to call Dr. Carling's office to see if she could check her out this morning."

Kelly set her coffee on the counter next to the grocery bag and bent down in front of Maggie, cradling her head in her arms. "What's the matter, old girl? You poor thing. Do you think she's in any pain?"

"I don't think so, but she does brush her paws over her eyes quite a bit, like it's irritating or something."

"You want me to come with?"

"Naw, you were up all night. I don't know for sure yet when she can even be seen."

A cancellation allowed Maggie to be seen by Dr. Carling at 10:15. She carefully examined Maggie and confirmed it was more than just cataracts. She measured pressures in Maggie's eyes and thought they were elevated although her instrument was not very sensitive. She was concerned that Maggie's smell was also gone and that her weight had dropped six pounds since her last visit. She found a couple of enlarged lymph nodes and did a needle biopsy. After looking at the slides under the microscope, Dr. Carling said the cells didn't look cancerous, but she would send the slides to the university to be read by a veterinary pathologist. She was worried that Maggie either had glaucoma or more likely a brain tumor of some sort. Dr. Carling recommended an appointment with a veterinary ophthalmologist and a CAT scan of her head. She doubted the blindness would be correctable regardless of the diagnosis. Dr. Carling talked about a third eyelid being up that indicated Maggie was probably in some pain. Jimmy was given a half dozen prednisone tablets to try to make her more comfortable until the further testing was done. On the ride home, Maggie lay on the seat with her head on Jimmy's lap instead of facing into the wind of the open window.

Jimmy left Maggie in the truck as he quietly walked into the house expecting Kelly to be asleep. She was up, puttering around in the kitchen.

"How'd it go?"

"Doesn't sound good. She thinks Maggie might have a brain tumor."

"That's awful. What did she think we should do?"

"Well, she recommended seeing a veterinary eye doctor and getting a CAT scan, but said it's unlikely they'll be able to treat whatever they find."

"What do you think we should do?"

"This place is dangerous for a blind dog. Maggie's always run loose, and I don't think she'd like being tied up or put in a kennel."

"Do you think we should put her down?"

"I don't know."

Kelly went into the bedroom and lay down while Jimmy got Maggie out of the truck and fed her a prednisone tablet rolled in a piece of deli turkey and took her for a walk down by the pond. She seemed perkier and followed his foot sounds pretty well. Maggie waded in the pond among the cattails while Jimmy lay back in the late morning sun. She seemed to be getting along better and Jimmy started thinking maybe she'd adapt to a sightless life on the farm. He watched her swimming ten to fifteen yards beyond the cattails, but noticed she was swimming in circles, not knowing which way to shore. Jimmy called her.

Maggie's ears perked, so he knew she heard him, but she seemed more anxious and disoriented, not sure exactly which direction the sound came from. Jimmy stripped down to his boxers and waded out in the frigid water to help Maggie back to shore. She was exhausted and panicky. As they made their way back to the house, he knew it was time to put her down.

Jimmy called Dr. Carling and although there weren't any openings, she told him to bring Maggie over any time and they could squeeze her in. Jimmy tied up Maggie to a large oak behind the house with her food and water nearby. When he went back into the house Kelly was at the kitchen table studying.

"What did you decide?" she asked without looking up.

Jimmy finished washing his hands in the kitchen sink and tossed the towel on the honey maple countertop. "I'm gonna take her in this afternoon have her put to sleep."

Kelly laid her book flat on the table and brought her eyes up to his. "How does that work? Do you keep the body or have it cremated or what?"

Jimmy remembered past family dogs put to sleep with a .22 slug to the temple, but figured he'd have trouble pulling the trigger on Maggie.

"Thirty dollars to put her asleep. Sixty-five to have her put asleep and cremated with a bunch of other animals and have the ashes buried somewhere in the township, ninety dollars if we want her ashes back so we can bury 'em ourselves."

"You want me to come with?" Kelly asked again.

"No, I'd just as soon go by myself."

As Jimmy untied Maggie, she came to her feet with more energy and tail wagging than earlier. When he opened the truck door, she tried to jump in and needed just a nudge from Jimmy to make it. As they started down the road her head was back out the window, nose into the wind. Jimmy had second thoughts. Maybe the prednisone was helping. Maybe it just took time to adjust. He took the long way into town. Jimmy turned down the radio as he pulled into a McDonald's drive-up. "Two cheeseburgers and a quarter-pounder with cheese."

As he drove, he opened one of the cheeseburgers, broke it up and fed it to a ravenous Maggie. He unwrapped the other cheeseburger and bit into his quarter-pounder as he turned left at the first stop light. Maggie found the unwrapped burger and wolfed it.

"Maggie...," Jimmy playfully scolded her as he finished the turn.

Gasping and choking sounds redirected Jimmy's attention as it became apparent that the burger was stuck in her throat. Jimmy pulled up to a residential curb, got out, and ran around to drag Maggie onto the boulevard. He tried to pull the burger out with his fingers, but it broke too easily, and he only managed to retrieve a bit of ketchup-stained bun and a pickle slice. He tried a Heimlich maneuver and was left with a dead dog in his arms as Maggie's body twitched, convulsed, turned rigid and finally went limp.

As he lifted her into the bed of the truck, he felt relieved that she at least had died of natural causes.

———————

Kelly watched from the kitchen window as Jimmy lifted Maggie's body out of the truck and into a wheelbarrow. He got a shovel from the barn and headed to the pasture. He used the shovel to lift the electric fence, as he pushed the wheelbarrow under it. Jimmy lifted his right leg over the fence and lowered it until his crotch almost touched the wire and then pushed off with his left foot and deftly swung it over. He wheeled out thirty or forty yards and dug the hole.

Maggie's body was put in along with a few items he pulled from his pockets. Half the dirt was shoveled back in. Jimmy crossed the fence again with the shovel and spaded up a three-foot cedar. The roots and encasing dirt were put into the lawn bag he pulled from his back pocket, and the tree was carried over the fence and placed into the hole. The rest of the dirt was packed around the tree and Jimmy stepped back to see if it was straight. He saw Kelly coming over with two five-gallon pails of water. He met her at the fence, took the buckets from her and poured them onto the tree. The buckets and shovel went into the wheelbarrow as he pushed it back toward Kelly.

"How you doin'?"

"Fine," Jimmy answered.

"Everything go okay?"

"Yeah, no problems."

"You up for a drive to the DQ for ice cream?"

Jimmy smiled. "You girls are all the same. Ice cream is the universal cure-all. Every time the sister of a high school buddy of mine broke up with her boyfriend, we'd find her up in her bedroom with her face buried in a bucket of butter pecan ice cream."

"So what's wrong with that? We learned in nursing school there's a chemical in ice cream that makes sadness go away."

"Yeah, right."

"I'm serious. Why do you think they always give it to kids after they have surgery?"

After a dozen silent steps and turning toward his truck, he agreed that "a chocolate chip cookie dough blizzard does sound pretty good."

Chapter Sixteen

William Curry had been sitting in a stuffed chair against the window when Frank got back from physical therapy late in the afternoon. With a waiting list for beds, the same day Richard Carlson moved out, Frank's new roommate had moved in. William was dressed in a formal blue Naval officer's uniform and had turned his head in Frank's direction without making eye contact as the therapist wheeled Frank into the room. A sixty-ish year old woman was carefully emptying the contents of a small suitcase into the dresser and closet. She greeted Frank and introduced him to William, who again looked toward, but not at, Frank.

"He likes to be called 'Captain.' He had a head injury in the South Pacific after the war, when a hurricane ripped through the island he was stationed on. His wife, my mother, was killed when the officer's quarters got torn apart. They found 'Captain' outside, unconscious, with coconuts scattered around him. They figured one must have struck his head and he was flown to the Naval hospital in Honolulu where he was in a coma for three weeks. The doctor said he didn't know if he'd wake up, and with the extent of his head injury, maybe he'd be better dead.

'Anyway, I've taken care of Daddy for over thirty years at home, and it just got to where I needed some help. He understands what he hears, but doesn't speak, hasn't since the hurricane." With that, she finished unpacking and left.

"Well, Captain, pleased to meet you. We all have our scars from the war." Realizing there wasn't going to be much dialogue, Frank left it at that.

Captain ate dinner with the other residents, needing help feeding himself and cleaning up afterward. At eight o'clock that first night and every night afterward, the daughter was back, helping Captain into his bedclothes and brushing his teeth. She took the uniform with her to be cleaned and pressed for the next day, arriving at 7:00 in the morning to help Captain out of his bedclothes, back into his uniform and back into the chair against the window. She always stayed until midmorning, talking to Captain, asking him how he liked his new home, how he felt, was he lonely, did he miss Mama?"

The answers to her questions came in the afternoons when she pulled an old instrument case out of the closet and carefully removed the saxophone that Captain had played in the Navy band. She gently placed it in his hands and brought the reed to his lips. For the next half hour, through the sax, he communicated to her beyond what words alone could have done. After precisely thirty minutes, he would lower the instrument and his daughter would take it from him, put it back into the case and back into the closet. She then would get Captain a pillow and make him comfortable for his afternoon nap in the chair and, after he had fallen asleep, she would leave, returning that evening to help him get ready for bed. This routine gave her the opportunity to stay involved with his care without the burden of meals and bathing.

Captain's saxophone quickly caught the attention of staff and residents alike. None of what he played was familiar to anyone and it was apparent that he was just playing the notes as they came to him. He not only conveyed his own thoughts, but seemed to capture the mood of the moment at Willow. He played rather droll melodies on the bad weather days or if there was more than the usual level of sickness or sadness, and more uplifting rifts when spirits were higher. As Christmas approached and the preparations of the advent season progressed, his music took on a sense of anticipatory excitement that spread throughout Willow Manor.

———————

A week after burying Maggie, Jimmy came in for breakfast with Kelly after milking and before she went to school. He'd finish chores after eating and planned to head over to the river in the afternoon for some late fall muskie fishing.

Why so quiet this morning? You having second thoughts about last night?" Kelly asked.

"No, not at all... did you know you got a lump on the right?" motioning toward her right chest.

"That's what you're worried about? Ah, yeah, that popped up a couple weeks ago. I figure it's just a cyst. Should go away on its own."

"Shouldn't you have it looked at?"

"I thought I'd give it another couple of weeks."

"Well, you know more about that stuff than I do, but it doesn't seem like anything to mess around with."

"Well, if it will make you feel better, I'll make an appointment to have it checked out, but I'm sure it's nothing. I'm only twenty-six. That's too young for it to be anything bad. Do you want to come with?"

"No, as long as you're sure it's nothing to worry about."

Jimmy had a good day on the river, landing two muskies greater than forty inches. After finishing milking, as he walked up toward the farmhouse, he was surprised that Kelly wasn't back from school yet. He enjoyed having her spend time out at the farm and found himself increasingly lonely when she wasn't there, especially now that Maggie was gone. As he opened the screen door, the sound of rubber on crushed gravel directed his attention toward the driveway as Kelly's car pulled in. He walked out to wait for her to pull up next to his truck. As she got out, she told him that she had been able to get an appointment at the clinic after school.

"How did it go?"

"Well, I saw a nurse practitioner first and she sent me to the surgeon who did an ultrasound in the office and told me it didn't look like a cyst, so she did a needle biopsy. I've got an appointment with her on Tuesday to go over the results."

"The surgeon? That doesn't sound good. Was she very suspicious?"

"I don't think so. She said it most likely was benign, but I do have a family history of breast cancer... two aunts, one died from it. They both had mastectomies when they were about fifty."

"So we won't know anymore until Tuesday?"

"No."

"Let's plan a bunch of stuff this weekend to take our minds off it."

Kelly didn't disagree.

Alice was half in the bag when Frank and Jimmy got back to the Mad Capper. They had split up, with Kelly and Alice staying at the bar while the guys went Christmas shopping. After cruising a few curio and antique shops and deciding to stay away from knickknacks and clothes, most of their time was spent at Sherman's Jewelers. Frank wanted to get something nice, but didn't want to spend much. He explained to Jeff, the owner, that neither he nor Alice were in very good health as he rolled a three-carat zirconium pendant in his fingers. Jeff gently teased the zirconium out of his hands and showed him a glistening tennis bracelet.

"If you saw Alice's hands, you wouldn't be trying to sell me anything to do with tennis."

"That's only what the style is called. They're really an everyday piece of jewelry." As Jeff described the piece in detail, Frank turned over the price tag, "Eighteen bucks, that's not bad at all."

"That's one thousand eight hundred dollars."

"Oh, well, like I said, neither of us are in very good health and probably won't be around long enough to enjoy it much and that's an awful lot of money," he said, reaching again for the zirconium.

"Who is this Alice?" Jeff asked.

After an abbreviated bio of Alice and how they had gotten to know each other, Jeff paused a moment before proceeding. "How 'bout leasing it for thirty bucks a month? Bring it back anytime. If you decide to buy it, just pay off the balance, no interest."

"I'll probably be the first of us to go. What happens then?"

"Alice's choice. Either she can bring it back or keep making the payments."

Frank ran the numbers in his head as to the cost if he died in three, six, or twelve months. Figured he'd most likely end up paying less than $400.

"Seems a little extravagant, but yeah, sure, I'll take it," he said, wondering if he should have tried to negotiate down the price.

As Jeff and Frank were completing the paperwork Jeff noticed Jimmy looking over the engagement rings. "Anything you want to see a little closer?"

"Uh, no, just waiting for you guys to finish up," he said, as Frank put the box into his coat pocket.

"So what have you girls been sippin' on?" Jimmy inquired, gesturing toward the empty martini glass in front of Kelly and a large water glass with an inch of brownish melted ice in the bottom. Also on the table was a platter that was empty except for a few remaining nachos smothered with chicken, cheese, beans, jalapenos, guacamole, and sour cream.

"Coupla cosmos for me," Kelly answered as Jimmy reached down to the platter and brought a mouthful to his face.

"Just a little iced tea," Alice slurred, leaving out the Long Island part and sliding her right hand over the wheelchair armrest and into Frank's lap, the palm of the crippled appendage rubbing his inner left thigh just below the groin.

Frank's mouth dropped a bit and his eyes scanned Jimmy and Kelly to see if they had noticed, which, of course, they had.

"Well, Alice, looks like it's our turn to hit the shops," Kelly said as she got up out of her chair and came around the table to help Alice out of hers.

The waitress came back, and Jimmy ordered a bottle of Dos Equis. Frank scanned the varied selection of tap beers, deciding to venture away from Leinenkugel's since it was a special occasion, ordering instead a Hacker Schorr.

"Damn good beer," Frank observed after the first swallow and before he and Jimmy ordered cheeseburger baskets. "What are you gonna get Kelly for Christmas?" he asked, having also noticed Jimmy perusing the rings.

"Haven't decided yet."

Kelly and Alice giggled like schoolgirls as they left the darkness of the bar and stepped into the bright sunlight bathing Main Street. They also found themselves at Sherman's Jewelers after browsing a couple of bookstores and art galleries.

After looking at a few watches, Alice asked, "what about an earring?"

"I'm not sure that's really Frank's style."

"So what? I'd love to see the look on his face when he opens it. He'd have no idea where to even put it."

"Speaking of which," Kelly commented as Jeff put a few plain gold earrings and a couple of diamond studs onto the counter, "maybe you'd like a belly button ring for yourself."

"Yeah, and I could get a couple nipple rings too and watch the three of 'em line up like the stars on Orion's belt."

Kelly's half plate of nachos nearly joined the jewelry on the countertop before she choked it back down. "Alice, you're too much. We should do this more often."

"I'd like that," she said, selecting a plain twenty-four karat gold earring for Jeff to ring up after negotiating a twenty-percent discount.

Chapter Seventeen

As Jimmy walked into the kitchen Monday afternoon, Kelly told him that the surgeon had called and said the lump was benign, a fibroadenoma.

"That's great, but I thought we weren't going to find out until tomorrow."

"I think if it had been bad news, she wanted to tell me in person. Anyway, she said we can just leave it alone unless I want it out."

"How big a deal is it to remove it?"

"Well, it's surgery, but she said it could be done under local anesthesia as an outpatient. Said the incision would be on the outer border of the areola, the dark skin around the nipple, so there wouldn't be much of a scar."

"Well, what do you think?"

"I don't know. Sounds like it's pretty elective, but I'm leaning toward having it taken out. It's kinda tender, and I just don't like having a lump there even though it's probably nothing to worry about."

"Well, it's up to you, but if it was me, I'd probably have it removed."

Changing the subject, Kelly asked, "What do you wanna do for supper?"

"I actually picked up a couple steaks and some veggies to throw on the grill."

"Nothing like a mid-December barbecue."

"Hey, high twenties today, almost balmy."

"Almost is right. If you do the grilling, I'll throw together a salad and open some wine."

"Sounds good," Jimmy said, as he exited the kitchen with charcoal and lighter fluid.

———

Both Jack and Kelly worked the 3 to 11 shift on Christmas Eve. Jack had spent the prior weekend doing Christmas with Jenny and his family at his sister's house. They would be at Jenny's parents' house Christmas Day until early afternoon when Jack conveniently would have to leave to go back to work another three-to-eleven shift. He would then drive back to Jenny's parents' home to spend the night. He had always gotten along fine with Jenny's mom, but her dad never thought Jack was quite worthy of his daughter, handicapped drama queen turned nurse working at an old folks home. Jack had told him that he was thinking about either applying to nurse anesthesia school or getting his master's in nursing administration. When that didn't make an impact, he had told his father-in-law that eventually he wanted to get his MBA in health care finance and work his way up the corporate ladder of a major for-profit hospital chain. This sparked an affirmative look that said, "Now, that's more like it" and a skeptical hand on the shoulder that said, "don't let me down." Two more years had gone by without his having taken the first step up the ladder, so Jack didn't exactly look forward to the get-togethers with Jenny's side of the family.

Kelly's family was spending Christmas at Sanibel, but Kelly had to stay back to work. They would all get together at her parent's home New Year's Day to eat and watch football with number boards on all the games. She had made arrangements to get off at 10:30 p.m. on Christmas Eve so she and Jimmy could go to the eleven o'clock candlelight service at her church, which was just four blocks from Willow.

Jimmy had stopped by the nursing home that morning with a six-foot balsam that he had cut down by the pond. Bringing the fragrant evergreen into Frank's room he screwed the threaded metal spike coming up from the bottom of the tree stand, an invention of a neighbor of his who owned a tree farm, into the 3/8" diameter hole he had drilled in the bottom of the tree. There were no brackets to tighten and no monofilament line running from the top of the tree to curtain rods to hold the tree in place.

After moving a few things around the balsam fit nicely in a corner by the window. Jimmy had brought in some tinsel, a string of blue lights and an old box of ornaments he had found in the hallway closet at the farmhouse. Frank and Alice took supper in Frank's room as they decorated the tree, first with the stuff Jimmy had brought and then added a few Styrofoam coffee cups with stapled yarn loops and the names of family members past and present written on the sides. They scattered fluffed up Kerlix gauze among the bows to look like clumps of snow. For the star they had pilfered a red light bulb off the lobby tree and swapped it with the last blue light bulb on the top of their own tree. They had Jack blow up a latex glove and tie it off with the red bulb inside it.

Neither Frank nor Alice could remember a finer star atop any Christmas tree they'd seen before. They listened to the KNXR Christmas Eve music program, played cribbage, ate caramel corn, and drank eggnog, which Frank had spiked with a little brandy from the bottom drawer. He had Jack hang some mistletoe from the ceiling earlier in the day, but forgot all about it and Alice didn't notice.

———————

Tillie Pillquist also took dinner in her room because she didn't want to miss the phone call from her son and daughter-in-law in California. Kelly had peeked into her room several times to see her sitting in her wheelchair, an arm's length from the phone, waiting, just waiting and staring out through nearly sightless eyes at a blurry world from which she had become disengaged. She thought of Christmases past; the best ones had been when her son was small, but the ones with his children were also memorable, before they had moved out-of-state, out-of-touch. The phone call never came, again. Kelly brought in some eggnog and turned on some Christmas music, which made it feel more like Christmas, but made it even more sad for Tillie because she was more aware that it was Christmas. Kelly did what she could to cheer Tillie up, but soon it was pushing ten o'clock which was well past Tillie's usual bedtime and she needed to finish her charting and change clothes to be ready when Jimmy came by.

Jimmy waited for Kelly in the nurse's break room, feeling awkward dressed in a new burgundy Christmas sweater with green holly woven into the front. He drank cheap coffee, mostly just for something to do while he waited. A melody drifting down the dim hallway lured him out of the break room and toward Frank's room, as nurses and patients also were pulled. They moved toward the sounds of a lone saxophone playing a familiar melody by a military man who, at the same time each Christmas Eve, played this particular song; the only melody familiar to the other residents or staff he would play all year. Kelly found Jimmy standing outside the Captain's room as he began the second of four stanzas of "Silent Night".

Willow was perfectly quiet except for the rich sound radiating from the sax. Jimmy scanned the menagerie of faces and the eyes within the faces in the hallway and inside the room, all captivated. He didn't notice Kelly standing by him, didn't perceive that she had noticed the lump in his throat as he mouthed along the remaining verses. A Christmas Eve feeling enveloped him with a peace he hadn't felt in a long time. Kelly did notice and thought of her grandmother's advice to not get involved with any guy who felt no emotion during "Silent Night" on Christmas Eve because there would be something missing. She slid over to put her hand in his, feeling transfer of the emotion of the music, of the night.

When the Captain finished, he lowered the sax from his lips to his daughter's hands. Kelly and Jimmy walked silently down the hall, through the lobby and courtyard into a windless, twenty-degree, mostly overcast, winter night with a few large flakes floating softly to the snow-covered ground. On their four block walk to the church, through a patch of clear sky, Kelly could see Orion. She looked at the belt, then out to the bow, back to the belt, thought of Alice, and laughed out loud.

"What's so funny?"

"Oh, nothing."

Self-conscious that it might have something to do with his new sweater, Jimmy left it at that. Kelly's eyes came back to the street, but her thoughts stayed with the three stars in the belt as she remembered being on the rooftop of her hotel in Puerto Vallarta with a guy from Argentina on the last night of a college spring-break trip. It was three o'clock in the morning as the Pacific lapped against the beach in front of them. They had met scuba diving and had been together for most of Kelly's last two days in Mexico. They spent the last hours before her flight home drinking Modelo at this unlikely, but perfect, spot with Fernando telling her the three stars were the *"Tres Marias."* She thought of herself flying thousands of miles north and of him flying thousands of miles south and the improbability of their ever seeing each other again despite talk of someday hiking together in Patagonia. Fernando had said when they were at home and looked up at the nighttime sky, at the *"Tres Marias,"* the southernmost star would be Argentina, the northernmost Minnesota, and the middle star would be the time they had together in Mexico.

It had been years since she had thought of Fernando, or that night, until this night, but it lingered with her as they walked to the church.

The candlelight service continued the mood of the evening, the closing hymn was the same as that played by the brain-damaged Captain back at Willow. It was accompanied by a piano, with the final verse a cappella, which brought the lump back to his throat so that he, again, faltered midway through the song.

After the service, as they walked downhill toward and then across Main Street, there was a flurry of cars leaving church parking lots and side streets; then it was quiet and still. They walked and talked their way out onto the lift bridge spanning the St. Croix River and stopped midway, facing downstream, leaning against the cast iron railing.

Kelly's mind retraced the evening; Tilly's loneliness, the relief from loneliness that Frank and Alice brought each other, the Captain's saxophone, the effect of that sax on Jimmy. There was the candlelight service, Orion's Belt, the beautiful snowflakes and now a pristine Christmas Eve night on a historic bridge with a guy who just might be *the guy*. It was all made more magical with a glowing half moon shining off the snow-covered river beneath them.

Chapter Eighteen

Jimmy's eyes scanned the Rockwellian wintry hillside of steeples and scattered lights to his right before bringing his gaze across the river to the Wisconsin side, with thoughts of backtrolling Rapalas over the rocks in ten feet of water for October walleyes just north of Hudson. His mind drifted further downstream, past Hudson to the mouth of the Kinnikinick River where he used to beach his boat and wade upstream in the crystal-clear waters casting for trout. His memory took him down river to where the clean, but tamarack-stained water of the St. Croix entered into the silty Mississippi near Prescott. He passed by the Cannon River bottoms north of Red Wing, where mallards had been called into spreads of decoys in backwater beaver ponds, and on to Red Wing and the annual carp fishing tournament sponsored by Andy's Bar.

The current carried him past Lake City with thoughts of Jack and

Fly and dead sheephead under a car seat on a hot summer's day. He thought of a Boy Scout camp north of Winona, where he and Bobby Richards had sneaked away from a warm early spring afternoon of working on merit badges to explore the shoreline of this greatest of all American rivers. The ice had recently broken up, and the river had been open, speckled with ice floes of varying sizes coming from the north and being carried downstream with the spring thaw. He and Bobby had been on an ice shelf off a point watching the floes pass by. Suddenly the tip of the shelf they were standing on broke off, and they found themselves adrift in the Mississippi a quarter mile from shore. They clung to a twenty-foot by ten-foot piece of ice, drifting as the sun passed through the barren hardwoods along a ridge on the west side of the Mississippi valley. It was late in the afternoon, and the temperature was dropping. They tried paddling the floe toward shore with their hands, but with the brisk current, they had succeeded only in getting their gloves and sleeves soaking wet without any effect on the floe's direction.

As darkness had nearly set in their rescue came in the form of an old man in an olive-green trench coat and fur hat who came out of nowhere in his fourteen-foot fishing boat. He loaded them up and took them back to his place on the river where they had warmed up by his wood-burning stove. His wife had made them hot chocolate and fresh out-of-the-oven peanut-butter cookies. The old man had given them a ride back to camp on Jimmy's last day of scouting.

Had Jimmy crossed the bridge and looked upstream, he would have been filled with even more memories. He'd think of canoeing the upper St. Croix and Namekagon Rivers, camping on the islands and sandy beaches, catching smallmouth bass, walleyes, muskie, and catfish at holes and reefs that had taken a good portion of his life to this point to discover. He'd remember jumping with his high school buddies from the bluffs by Taylor's Falls and the time his truck at the marina wouldn't start, so he ordered a pizza delivery to the farm. The Dominos was just a couple blocks away. When he got there, he waited outside and asked the delivery guys where they were going. The driver going to the farm agreed to take him along although he "really wasn't supposed to". The Dominos special was two medium pizzas for eight dollars, so for ten bucks, he got a ride home, a pizza for both Frank and him, and a two-dollar tip for the driver. This river system had been his playground, and he appreciated being near it on this night, even though it was under a couple of feet of ice and snow.

"These last three months have been a lot of fun," Kelly began.

"Yeah, I don't think I've had a better fall myself... except for maybe my senior year in high school when I went duck hunting out near the Dakotas with a buddy of mine, and the bluebills came through so thick you...."

"Don't even start."

"What I meant to say was getting to know you was the best thing that's happened to me."

"That's more like it. So, what's next?"

"What's next?"

"Yeah, so where do we go from here?" Kelly asked.

"Ahh, back to your place and roll around on the couch for a while?"

"Ha, ha. You know what I mean."

Jimmy had hoped the night would proceed in this direction, but was somewhat surprised that it actually did. He could feel the chill of the frozen walkway transmitted through his flimsy loafers, dulling the sensation from his toes. He began slowly, choosing his words carefully.

"Well, there's nothing I enjoy more than spending time with you and have thought a lot about taking our relationship to the next level of commitment." Jimmy studied her eyes and could tell she was puzzled with his opening. "With just the two of us there's always plenty of room, we don't feel crowded, we do lots of stuff together, but we also can do things on our own. I'm worried that pretty soon the truck won't seem big enough and we'll be trading it in for a minivan."

Kelly laughed briefly and watched Jimmy's face for a smile. She thought she knew his sense of humor, but this seemed different. "What the hell does a minivan have to do with it?"

"Well, all my married friends gave up almost everything after getting married. When I do get together with them, which isn't very often anymore, they never have much time. They seem distracted, they complain about their wives and mostly just talk about their kids and how they race from one event to another, or what new mutual funds they're putting money into. They're out of shape, they gobble antacids and generally seem miserable... but they all have shiny new minivans. No thanks."

"So you're gonna spend the rest of your life by yourself in a boat or a cow barn with the high times being when you can drive around in that piece of shit truck of yours listening to the radio. Excuse me for suggesting that I might want to be a part of your life, 'cause I don't."

With that Kelly started walking back across the bridge toward town.

That wasn't exactly how Jimmy had hoped the night would end and wondered how it had. He had gotten a ride to Willow Manor from a neighbor who was coming into town. Kelly knew he didn't have his truck and he was surprised she didn't at least offer to give him a ride home. Jimmy stood and watched her until she was out of sight. Pulling the small box from his pocket, he opened it and in the dim light could see a sparkle from the diamond engagement ring he had sold his truck to buy. Kelly thought the truck was up on blocks back in the barn when it was actually sitting in a used-car lot in White Bear Lake.

Closing the box and putting it back into his pocket, Jimmy headed across the bridge and up the mile-long hill on the Wisconsin side. There would be no Dominos delivery guy to give him a ride home tonight. The only vehicle he saw was a semi pumping its brakes in the westbound lane as it came down the hill toward the bridge. The trucker had been on the road the past three days, and looked across the river at the lights of his hometown. It was a tough time of year to be on the road, but he would be home for Christmas.

Jimmy's farmhouse was ten miles of winding country road away. The sky had mostly cleared, but the temperature had not dropped as much as would have been expected. The air was still with the only sounds being his loafers crunching the crusted snow into the gravel as he walked.

In every direction, multicolored light displays pronounced the season. The first couple of hours he could see lights on in some of the homes and, through a few front windows, he could see fathers moving about as they scrambled to finish putting together the "some assembly required" toys. Then the homes went dark except for the outside displays.

Christmas carols from the candlelight service replayed in Jimmy's head and he hummed along to "Silent Night." He saw no vehicles; all was calm; the stars were bright.

Toward morning, lights began coming on in the homes and through a few front windows he could see excited kids in bright-colored pajamas and tired-looking parents in bathrobes. He thought back to his own Christmases as a kid, the ones before his mother had died and his father had started drinking. They had been everything Christmas should be for a kid. They had oyster stew and prime rib every Christmas Eve before church. He'd wake up Christmas morning, having no recollection of falling asleep on the drive home from church and being carried into the house by his father. It would take a few sleepy moments before he was awake enough to remember what day it was and race downstairs, hoping his sister hadn't beaten him to the tree. Years later he would realize that his parents really hadn't had the means to be buying the presents he and his sister Sarah got those years, but it explained why his dad seemed to be working a lot and always seemed tired.

His mind skipped ahead a few years, to after his dad had died, when he had moved out to the farm with Frank and Betty and his sister had moved to California to live with an aunt. He was older then and Christmas hadn't seemed as big a deal. He and Frank would usually buy each other fishing tackle. Betty would buy him clothes and he'd buy her the same lotion every year. His best hunting boots were a pair that Frank had surprised him with four years ago, his second Christmas without Betty.

His thoughts were interrupted by the bellowing of his Holsteins, which could be heard a full mile away. He was late for milking and they weren't happy about it. He went straight to the barn, pulled his overalls over his church clothes, did the milking and a few chores. By midmorning he was out cold on his bed, fully clothed, no breakfast. Shortly after noon, the phone woke him with a neighbor calling to let him know his cows had gotten out again.

Chapter Nineteen

Christmas Day entertainment at Willow was a string quartet that played in the lobby for a couple of hours, with holiday punch and frosted sugar cookies during a mid-performance break. The quartet was led by 91-year-old violinist Herman Meyer who had played professionally with the Minneapolis Symphony until his hearing went bad at age 75. He and his now 90-year-old wife had moved to Minneapolis in 1941 because he couldn't get a job with any of "the big three" - the symphonies in New York, Boston, or Philadelphia. Shortly after moving, however, he had been drafted in the Air Force and was stationed in England as a communications specialist for most of the war.

Upon returning to Minnesota, he rejoined the Minneapolis Symphony and "never worked an honest day after that." The symphony season initially lasted six months, but he would scratch out enough to live on by playing social events the remainder of the year, mostly in quartets.

Since retiring, he continued to play as often as he could get the other strings together, whether or not they had an audience. His hearing had declined to where he was playing "mostly by feel, like that Tommy guy who plays pinball by sense of smell." He had otherwise remained in excellent health. He and his wife, who was also in good health, lived independently at an upscale assisted living complex where music and socializing remained an integral part of their lives. Herman's latest project had been spending two years writing a history of the Minneapolis Symphony to commemorate its one-hundredth anniversary.

Frank and Alice had exchanged presents the night before. Alice beamed at the attention she got from her new tennis bracelet while Frank was a bit self-conscious about the gold ring piercing his left ear. After the performance, they had chatted with Herman and Helga for a while, which got them invited to a dinner party at the Meyer's on New Year's Eve, complete with live music and dancing. Frank and Alice readily accepted the offer, with Alice already concerned as to whether she had anything to wear to such an event.

By late afternoon, the Holsteins were back in the pasture, the tree that had fallen on the fence had been removed and the fence had been repaired. Crashing again on the couch, Jimmy was woken by the bawling cows, again not happy about being milked late. Jimmy made a sandwich on the way to the barn. On the way back to the house he noticed headlights coming down the driveway and recognized his truck.

A deal is a deal, he thought, expecting to see the used car guy wanting his money back. As the truck pulled closer, he saw that Kelly was driving. The smooth-running engine quieted, the headlights turned off and the driver side door swung open with Kelly climbing down from the cab.

"How did you get the truck?" Jimmy asked, taking a few steps toward her.

"Frank told me why you didn't have it last night. I was able to track down the dealer at his home, and told him what happened. He met me at the dealership this afternoon. I traded him my Saturn for the truck, plus a couple thousand bucks."

"I can't believe he would do that on Christmas Day. Can't believe you would do that anytime. You traded your Saturn for it? How are you going to get around?"

"How were you planning to get around when you sold your truck to buy the ring in the first place?"

"I didn't really think about it. It just seemed like what I needed to do. I figured it would all work out in the end."

"You just answered your own question. Do you still have the ring?"

"Yeah, why?"

"Oh, I just wanted to see if it fits."

"What if it does?"

"Well, if there's a question that goes along with it, the answer would be 'yes.'"

"Hey, I'm pretty tired; please don't tease me," Jimmy said.

"I'm not teasing."

"You're serious? About getting married?"

"Very," Kelly replied.

"This day just got a whole lot better." As Jimmy moved toward Kelly, he stopped. "These are pretty disgusting," motioning toward his manure-stained overalls.

"If it bothered me, I wouldn't be here."

The ring fit perfectly; and when their lips met under the farmyard light, it was a moment beyond game six and fifty-inch muskies.

"I don't really have much for dinner, just frozen pizza and Sara Lee cheesecake. I do have some Mogen David and a few Leinies left."

"Uh, actually, I picked up a few things for dinner on the way out here and grabbed a bottle of pretty decent champagne. I also have your Christmas present in the truck," she said, walking back to the passenger side, opening the door, and pulling out a wiggling, squealing black ball of fur. "Black lab, good papers, and his mother seemed like a great family dog. I was going to give him to you at my apartment last night, but... well, anyway I thought we could call him Captain after Frank's roommate. Merry Christmas."

The lump from the night before returned to Jimmy's throat as he held Captain and beheld the moment. "It certainly is."

Unloading Kelly's travel bag, the groceries and champagne from the front seat of the truck and walking up to the house Jimmy wondered why a girl like Kelly would choose to spend the rest of her life with a guy like him.

Jimmy's arms were full as they reached the farmhouse door. Opening it for him, Kelly suggested that maybe the next day they could go kick tires on a few minivans. She promptly let Jimmy know that she was just kidding, although Jimmy actually would have been okay with the idea.

On New Year's Eve Jimmy and Kelly dropped Frank and Alice off at the Meyers on their way to Minneapolis to meet a few of Kelly's nursing school friends for dinner. Alice had called Helga regarding how to dress for the party and had been told to "go for it," which increased Alice's anxiety because of her rather limited wardrobe. Kelly stepped in and, tapping into her mother's friends, put together a stunning black silk ensemble with a sable stole for Alice, and a black tux complete with tails for Frank. With a little coaxing, Frank agreed to wear the earring and Alice's bracelet accented her outfit superbly.

Not surprisingly, a string quartet was the featured entertainment. During the pre-dinner socializing, Frank and Alice found a lot in common with a group of vigorous individuals their age and older, several of whom had also arrived in wheelchairs. Herman stopped the music once to welcome the fourteen guests and make a few announcements, including seating arrangements for dinner. The only rule he said was that there could be no mention for the entire evening of any illness, disability, or medical condition. There would be a medi-van arriving at one o'clock to give all who needed it a ride home.

The event was fully catered with a flamboyant kitchen staff, a stud-muffin bartender, and a voluptuous, surgically enhanced waitress. The champagne flowed freely, and the appetizers were elegant. Dinner came in courses with a wine steward describing and pouring a different glass of Italian with each course. The entrees were a succulent beef tenderloin and buttery sea scallops that were, as Frank later told Jimmy, "the size of urinal discs." Dessert was an apple tart topped with cinnamon ice cream. All sixteen diners were seated at one long table with Herman and Helga on opposite ends.

The conversations had been lively, with perspectives shaped by two World Wars, two lesser wars, a cold war, a depression, the advent of a space program, major developments in transportation, communications, and medicine, as well as evolving trends in music, politics, social issues, fashion, and earth ecology. There had been a toast to Ben Franklin who "did more for our country and fathered more children after age seventy than most American heroes did in a lifetime."

The quartet resumed after dinner and, with arthritic joints loosened by the grape, the dancers took to the makeshift dance floor with vigor and style. Alice and Frank weren't so much dancing as just holding each other up to the music, but it didn't matter. Noisemakers had been passed out and glasses filled ten minutes before the countdown with "Old Lang Syne" played on Herman's stereo. There were hugs, kisses, and handshakes all around; everyone fully aware this was probably the last New Year's Eve for at least a couple of the guests.

Frank and Alice embraced on the dance floor after a lengthy kiss, savoring the moment as Herman played "Old Lang Syne" for the third time.

It had been a wonderful evening, but the highlight came a half hour after midnight. The strings had left, and Herman was playing some big band CDs on his stereo with a two-hundred-watt amp and "kick-ass speakers." His deafness had him repeatedly turning up the volume with Helga following behind and turning it down. The decibels of the music and the laughter continued to rise until a firm knock on the front door quieted the place. Turning down the music, Herman opened the door to reveal a security officer who looked as surprised as the guests.

With more than a trace of sheepishness, he told Herman that they had received several complaints and asked him to try to keep it down. Herman had promised he would do his best and, as the door closed, a collective cheer broke loose from a group in which none had been to a party broken up by the police in over fifty years.

The only untoward occurrence of the evening occurred when Henry Johanson had a fainting episode and went down like a sack of potatoes on the dance floor from a cardiac arrhythmia. Helga had the phone in her hand ready to dial 911 when Henry's wife motioned her to put the phone down, saying that Henry "does this all the time, like a damned possum - gets too excited and just blacks out." She said if they just put him on the couch for a few minutes, he'd be okay. They did, and he was.

The night ended as Jimmy and Kelly picked Frank and Alice up at the same time that a few tipsy party-goers were being helped into the medi-van.

Chapter Twenty

Per family tradition, Kelly spent New Year's Day at her parents' house, with Jimmy joining them in the afternoon after morning chores and a visit to Willow. Kelly broke the news to her family - who adored Jimmy - shortly after Jimmy's arrival, which prompted a champagne toast. Kelly's mother made a few phone calls. By late afternoon the date was set for a September wedding and the church and country club had been reserved.

By that evening, her mother already had a lengthy invitation list and was overflowing with ideas for the service, the reception and even the honeymoon. Her father's attempts to cool her mother's jets were to no avail, with Kelly initially enjoying her mother's excitement, but later having to bite her tongue lest she burst her mother's bubble, knowing there would be opportunity later to reassert her ideas into the wedding plans while apologizing to Jimmy for her mother's overinvolvement.

"Well, the way I figure it, the more she does, the less we have to do and I'm hoping they plan on paying for a good portion of it because I don't think we can afford what your mom's talking about."

"They said a long time ago they'd pay for half of my college and most of my wedding, so I don't think that'll be a problem."

"I do have some ideas for the honeymoon and do want to set that up myself."

"Oh, yeah, what did you have in mind?" she said with a bit of tease in her voice.

"You'll have to wait and see, but I think you'll like it."

His thoughts shifted to the reception, wondering how his friends would fit in at her parents' country club and observing that his invitation list of relatives and friends would be pretty short.

Moving into the four-season porch, their conversation shifted to where they would live.

"The farm is almost paid for, and Frank told me he's giving me the whole quarter section. With the development going on south of our place, land prices are going up and we should be able to get a good price for it, which would get us off to a pretty decent start."

"Sell the farm? I thought we'd be living out there. I love that place. Any stresses or baggage I leave the city with just melt away as I drive out." She thought of those warm days with the breeze just right when she would open the car windows to savor the pungent, but earthy and honest smells of recently spread manure. She also cringed, just a bit, at the thought of having to roll up those same windows to avoid the pungent, but putrid down-wind air coming from a corporate pig farm.

"I just assumed you'd want to live in the city, closer to work and your family.

"Believe me, the farm is close enough to both."

"Well, I have another idea I was thinking about if you did want to live out there. I do want to sell off the dairy operation. It's just not practical anymore to do mom-and-pop milking. There are dairy farms out by us that are milking over five hundred cows, milking twenty-four hours a day with migrant labor. They have calves being born year-round by artificial insemination - no need for bulls anymore. They all get banded into steers when they're born. Every once in a while, they get a band that doesn't take and they end up with a one-nutter that has some bull left in him, but he doesn't get near the cows anyway."

"My old boyfriend should have been steered," Kelly joked.

"The size of the cropping is getting bigger too. A lot of the land out there is owned by a family in St. Paul that made a ton of money in software and are now buying land on the cheap from farmers going bankrupt. This year I heard they've got in thirty-five hundred acres of corn and fifteen hundred acres of beans along with milking three-hundred head. They've got a big ass John Deere that's a sixteen-row planter and holds four hundred fifty gallons of fuel. It's no secret that they're only holding the land until the developers are willing to pay their price, which will probably be over $10,000 an acre. Takes a lot of buck-eighty corn, with expenses eating up most of that, to make ten grand. Just a business transaction, no real connection to the land itself."

Jimmy continued, "a friend of mine who trout fishes in Montana said the same thing is happening out there with out-of-state money buying up the ranches and driving up the property taxes so the legitimate ranchers can't make it."

"If that's happening around the country, where is our food gonna come from?" Kelly asked.

"I don't know, more chemicals and genetics, more reliance on developing countries and maybe some creative approaches like hydroponics, but a way of life that helped define our country will be gone."

"So what's your plan?"

"I'll show you some drawings I made when we get back tonight."

Chapter Twenty-One

Frank and Alice had slept in after their big night, missing breakfast. Both were finally awakened by skeletal pain, Alice from
the arthritis and Frank from the bony metastasis from the prostate
cancer, which had progressed despite the Lupron. The excitement
and wine of the night before had given them a reprieve, but now they
were both pushing buttons for the nurses to bring them the pain pills,
which allowed them to carry on in four-hour increments.

Later that week, Frank would start on a narcotic patch that got
changed every three days and delivered a steady dose of pain relief
which worked better than the pills.

———————

At the farmhouse Jimmy grabbed a beer out of the fridge and

poured Kelly a glass of chablis before pulling a two-by-three-foot tag board down from the top of a bookshelf. "Here's our one hundred and sixty acres. I'd like to keep twenty including the pond, a few acres of woods and some of the better pasture so we could still keep some Angus."

"They're the all black, muscular beef cows, right?" she said.

"Yep," Jimmy smiled. "So here's where I thought the house could go, great spot for a walkout to the pond."

Flipping the tag board over, he showed Kelly a floor plan with detailed drawings of a ranch-style rambler with a deck off the kitchen overlooking the pond and above the walkout patio below.

"I didn't know you could draw like this. These are great."

"I've always liked drawing and seem to have a knack for it. I would actually like to go back to school to study architecture."

"Looks like you'd be good at it. You're always surprising me with something. That's what I like about you."

"And I thought it was my dancing."

"That too," she agreed, directing her focus back to the tag board. "Five bedrooms?" Kelly asked.

"Well, we'd want a nice guest room, and the kids should have their own rooms."

"So three bedrooms means three kids, huh?" Kelly said with a laugh; she was surprised at the time and thought he had put into this.

"Well, you seem to like kids. I don't know how many we'd want or end up with, but three kids' bedrooms seemed like a good start."

"Are there many kids around here?"

"A few. There's a couple developments not too far from here and unfortunately it looks like there may be more on the way."

"What school system is this?"

"Somerset."

"That's where the Apple River tubing parks are, aren't they? We went there a couple times back in high school. It got pretty wild in the campgrounds."

"Yeah, it got rowdy enough a few years ago that they tried to ban alcohol on the river, thinking they could still make it with just families and church groups, but nobody came so they changed it back to how it was. Just too much money to be made. Same way with the outdoor concerts."

"Yeah, we went to a couple of those too, an Oz Fest and an Edge-Fest. Both times we camped out in the rain. It was a mess, but the mosh pit was an experience."

"With the Apple River, the concerts and a couple strip bars, the town hasn't had the best reputation, but I think that's changing. The local politics had been controlled by a French mafia - a half dozen families that have used bribery, threats, and arson to get what they want. There's a lot of new people moving into the area trying to change that. They just built an indoor hockey rink and are putting more money into the schools. We're seeing a few different faces on the village council. I think it's gonna be a great place for us to live and for our kids to grow up."

"What about Frank?"

"I was thinking about him too. There certainly is enough room in this house for him to move back, and now that there's two of us, especially with you being a nurse, I think we could manage."

"He'd never leave Alice."

"I know. I think there'd be room for her too."

"What if they wanted to sleep together?"

"Well," Jimmy responded in a very parental tone, "all we can do is try to set a good example. There comes a point where you just have to let go and hope they make good choices."

"Yeah, some example! Speaking of, I got bored stiff watching football today and all I could think about was you. I grabbed a couple bottles of my parents' wine and a few candles on the way out. I thought we could fill up the tub and work on that example we're setting."

"I'll get the water going."

It took very little coaxing to get Frank and Alice to agree to move out to the farm; their primary hesitations were leaving the nurses who had become friends as well as caregivers, and a concern about cramping Kelly and Jimmy at a time when their life together was just beginning. The latter concern was quickly dispatched, and plans were made to move the following week. Alice had been out to the farmhouse a couple of times before. She and Kelly talked over some basic decorating and furniture rearranging, choosing which of the two remaining bedrooms she and Frank would share. Jimmy and Jack spent that Saturday building a wheelchair ramp up to the back door with access to a west-facing deck. A going-away party at Willow preceded the medi-van trip out to the farm, with Jimmy and Kelly leading the way in the truck, Frank and Alice's belongings in boxes in the back.

Frank had retained vivid visual memories of the farm, but had forgotten how much he missed the sounds and the smells. Alice transitioned smoothly and noticed lessening of her rheumatoid pain almost immediately, gaining enough mobility to where she was able to help in the kitchen and with housekeeping to a limited extent. Home-care nurses were welcome visitors three times a week, as winter rolled into spring and as Frank's prostate cancer progressed, providing them assistance with issues of pain control, nutrition, and bowel function.

Despite the continued decline, Frank had some good days when, for whatever reason, his energy level picked up, his breathing was easier, and the pain subsided. He would generally know it was going to be a good day as soon as he woke in the morning and, with Alice still asleep, he would dress himself and wheel out to the barn before Jimmy finished milking, invigorated by the fresh air on the way to the barn and the activity within it, proudly watching his grandson's deft handling of the milking process and taking further pride in the new life Jimmy was creating for himself. Mid-morning on those good days would find Jimmy wheeling Frank back up to the farmhouse with Kelly having left for school in the truck and Alice doing her best to get started on making breakfast.

On one of those good mornings as Jimmy wheeled him back to the house, Frank said, "That's quite a girl you've got, Jimmy."

"Thanks for getting us together. I doubt any of this would have happened if it wasn't for you."

Frank intentionally changed the subject by pointing across the barren snow-crusted field and reminded Jimmy that the homestead behind the distant shelterbelt was the old Torgerson place. "They had a kid that went to school with your dad. They played ball together," he said, his voice trailing off.

The evenings on those good days were even better as Jimmy walked alone from the barn to the house, the sun setting over his right shoulder, Frank and Alice arm in arm on the deck taking in those precious last rays, Kelly home from school working the dirt in neglected gardens around the farmhouse - gardens that would soon begin exploding with color, Captain racing in circles at Jimmy's feet.

On those spring evenings, on Frank's good days, as Jimmy walked toward the farmhouse, he would slow it down, letting Frank and Alice on the deck, Kelly in the garden, Captain at his feet and the sun over his shoulder melt into him as he walked, savoring it, knowing it was transient. If the breeze was coming from the northwest, the moment often included a train whistle, Frank no longer asking the question, Alice no longer giving the destination.

Chapter Twenty-Two

"**H**is blood count was pretty low. They figure that's why he was getting so tired and short of breath this past week. He's in the hospital getting a transfusion and preparing him for a colonoscopy tomorrow to see if they can find where the bleeding is coming from. Jimmy stayed with him," Kelly explained to Alice.

"He'd been doing so well before that. Is it anything to worry about?"

"We'll know more tomorrow. I'm going back over tonight. You want to come with?"

"If you don't mind hauling me around," Alice said.

"Don't be silly. Frank didn't like having to go to the hospital. It'll cheer him up to have you there."

The second unit of blood was hanging when Kelly and Alice entered Frank's room. He was getting the transfusion slowly and with an intravenous diuretic after each unit of blood, to lessen the risk of putting him into heart failure from too much fluid. He appeared to be sleeping as they peeked in the room, but opened his eyes and looked toward them as they entered. He tried a couple of wrong buttons on the bed railing before finding the one that raised him up.

"You didn't have to come over," he directed toward Alice.

"There wasn't much going on at the farm, so I just thought I'd tag along. How are you feeling?"

"Better. I guess my tank was a couple pints down. Just needed a refill."

"How low was it?" Alice asked.

"What did they say it was?" he asked, turning toward Kelly.

"A little over six. Should be thirteen or fourteen," she said.

"That is low. And you never noticed any sign of bleeding?" Alice inquired in a skeptical tone.

"No," Frank responded defensively. "Stools may have been a little darker than usual, but no blood at all."

Changing the subject, but still with a surprisingly firm tone, she asked, "What time is the colonoscopy?"

"I think it'll be around ten."

Softening up a bit, she said, "well, we'll just have to see what turns up, hopefully it's nothing serious."

"Yeah, I think this old car has enough problems without anything new."

————————

Jimmy arrived at the hospital at nine o'clock in the morning and walked along as Frank was taken by wheelchair to the endoscopy suite. The procedure was explained, including the medications he would receive through his IV to take the edge off. Jimmy was told he could stay and watch on the video screen, but he chose to wait in the lobby.

He grabbed an old issue of National Geographic and began thumbing through it. Half an hour later he heard his name called and the volunteer at the reception desk pointed to the conference room where the gastroenterologist would meet him. Dr. Pizini stepped in a few minutes after Jimmy had sat down in a brick-red leather sofa chair next to a corner table.

"Anybody else?" Dr. Pizini began. He was just shy of six feet tall, looked to be in his mid-fifties with thinning gray hair, and thick-framed chocolate brown glasses on a jowly St. Nick-like face, which had broken into effortless smiles prior to the procedure. Jimmy thought he seemed more serious and his smile, on entering the room, seemed a bit forced.

"No, just me," Jimmy answered.

Sitting on a matching chair adjacent to Jimmy's, Dr. Pizini continued, "Frank did fine. He tolerated the procedure and medication without a problem. I was able to get all the way around."

Then, after a short pause and with more direct eye contact, he said, "I think we found the reason for his low blood count."

Another pause.

"Frank has a large tumor in the right side of his colon. I took a few biopsies and the pathologist confirmed that it's cancer. It's close to where the small bowel empties into the large bowel and looks to be fairly large, almost obstructing.

"Has Frank had any bloating or cramping, trouble eating, moving his bowels, lost any weight?"

"He hasn't said anything, but that doesn't mean he hasn't had any of those. He probably wouldn't tell us if he did. Last thing he wants is any more problems that put him back in the hospital or nursing home."

"Well, I think he's going to need surgery. It's not something that chemo or radiation will be very effective for. Because of the size, I've ordered a CT scan of his abdomen for this afternoon to look for any spread of tumor. The chest x-ray they took last night looked okay. I'll have the surgeon come by tomorrow morning to talk it over with you.

He'll probably come before eight o'clock."

"I haven't told Frank any of this yet and was going to tell him now. Do you want to come with?"

Distracted by a myriad of fleeting thoughts, Jimmy refocused, "Huh, oh, yeah. I do."

Chapter Twenty-Three

That evening, while a 15-year–old boy with acute appendicitis was being transferred to the OR, positioned and put to sleep Dr. Steven Payne reviewed Frank's chart, endoscopy report, pathology, and CT scan. He planned to see the 82-year-old fellow the following morning before starting his elective surgery schedule. The staging CT had shown metastatic spread to his liver. Dr. Payne also looked through the man's past medical and social history as well as his medications. Dr. Pizini had told him that both Frank and his grandson knew about the colon cancer, but not the CT results.

Dr. Payne performed the straightforward laparoscopic appendectomy while a team from the Red Cross harvested tissue in the adjacent operating room from a 34-year-old pregnant woman who had died suddenly of a massive blood clot to her lung. After talking to the boy's family, dictating the operative report, and writing post-op orders, he had scribbled down a few thoughts on a blank progress sheet to try to put a handle on the intangible:

9 o'clock at night

Routine appy in my room

But next door...

The Red Cross is harvesting

bone, corneas and heart valves

from...

a 34-year-old

24-week pregnant

female...

wife...

mother-to-be...

that died today

blood clots to her lung that...

robbed her of the oxygen...

she needed to

keep living to

give birth to

their first child...

new members at our church a couple months ago

husband was a patient of mine, hernia repair

nice guy...

How do you deal with

losing your wife and first child

at the same time...

when out of the blue

blood clots go to her lungs

and... rob her of oxygen

and... she dies... they die?

The anesthetist for my case

helped with her resuscitation

that was... unsuccessful... and he

is still pretty shook up... nurses had to leave early

because

they were too shook up to

keep working... after

the blood clot went to her lungs

and robbed her of the oxygen...

The appendix wasn't ruptured so my patient

will probably go home tomorrow and will be okay

but...

what about the husband who lost his wife and first

child today?

Shortly after arriving home from the appendectomy, he had been called back to the emergency department to consult on a 12-year-old boy with a ruptured spleen from a skateboard accident. The kid was stable, and Dr. Payne felt that Casey, like most kids with busted spleens, could be managed without surgery, but would need to be watched in the hospital for a couple of days. While he was doing the boy's admit orders, the ER doctor had showed him the x-ray of an elderly fellow from town who had come in by ambulance because of a sudden onset of severe abdominal pain. The x-ray showed a large amount of air in the abdomen outside of the intestines, suggestive of a perforated bowel.

Owen Samuelson's medical history included arthritis for which he took a lot of anti-inflammatory medications. After talking with and examining the fellow Dr. Payne called the charge nurse and told her to call in the OR crew for a perforated ulcer. It had been just after two in the morning when he finished patching the perforation with a portion of the fatty apron that lies over the intestines, closing the incision, doing the post-op orders, dictating, and talking to the family. On the way home he thought about the kid with appendicitis, the old man with the perforated ulcer, the kid with the ruptured spleen, the woman with the blood clot and her husband.

He then thought about his last patient in clinic that day and a smile turned to a laugh as he recalled his nurse warning him that, "this one's a little different," as she gave him the patient's chart outside the exam room.

The elderly woman had been bothered by irregularity of her bowels and thought it might be helpful to bring in an album with pictures of every bowel movement she had taken over the past month, each one accompanied by a story as though she were showing him an album of her grandchildren. He had done pretty well keeping a straight face until he thought of the employee at the photo lab who had processed the pictures. She had gotten a colonoscopy within the past year so he just told her to push the fiber and fluids. He thought of how unglamorous his job could be at times - often revolving around stool, pus, blood, bile, urine, vomit and mucous.

After two hours of uninterrupted sleep, he was called by the ER doctor again, with a 55-year-old man with a plastic toothbrush travel case stuck in his rectum that could be felt but not removed. The doctor had tried several different clamps, but they kept slipping off as he tried to pull the inch-wide plastic cylinder through the anal sphincters. Dr. Payne had told them to move the patient to the endoscopy room and have the sigmoidoscope and jumbo polyp snare set up.

The all-too-familiar late-night trip to the hospital brought back memories of his surgical residency where time without sleep was measured not in hours, but in nursing shifts, often seeing the same group of nurses coming in for their third shift without having had any meaningful sleep in between. They had had no cross-coverage at his residency program, so the residents were always on call for their own patients twenty-four hours a day, seven days a week. It made for good continuity of patient care, but the busier surgical services would force the residents to essentially move into the hospital, their call rooms taking on the look of studio apartments with half-hearted attempts at adding a personal touch with pictures, lamps, clock radios, textbooks, and other items. It was easier for the single residents who generally made little attempt to have a life outside the hospital, but was tough on the married residents for whom keeping the beginnings of a family together had become a secondary focus.

There had been tremendous camaraderie among the diverse group who had become his fellow residents, sharing moments that ranged freely from exhilarating to devastating. Breakfast was always rushed and lunch nonexistent, but dinner was more relaxed. After finishing with the elective surgical cases for the day and presenting any new in-hospital consults to the attending staff, they would often spend upwards of an hour at the dinner table. It was a special time of kicking back, recalling the day's events, and commiserating before starting the night's work of rounding on the service patients, checking on any lab and x-rays that had been done during the day, doing discharge planning, reviewing the charts, reading up on the procedures and pathology for the patients scheduled for surgery the next day and responding to any nursing questions, family concerns or new consults.

Those on trauma call would be covering the ER and taking emergent surgical patients to the operating room. The residents on the busier services would be spending another night at the hospital, while others would hustle through what had to be done so they could take off, sometimes home and sometimes to the hospital library to prepare case presentations for the weekly residents' teaching conference or the monthly morbidity and mortality conference. On a good day, the conference was two parts educational and one part confessional, a bad day had the residents taking the fall for complications on the attending's patients. More often than not, the junior residents who had gotten out of the hospital would end up at one of the downtown bars or at a nurse's party, regardless of how tired they were.

Driving along, he remembered the hike from the call rooms to the surgical ICU, which was two buildings away in the fragmented eleven-hundred-bed hospital where he had spent most of his time. He recalled a particular surgical service as a junior resident when night after night he had been responsible for a dozen or so of the sickest patients in the hospital, just trying to keep them all alive until morning rounds. He remembered the ever-present Styrofoam cup of cheap coffee in his hand, the peacefulness of the ICU at night with the background of softly beeping monitors and hushed voices, the families either out of the hospital or asleep on makeshift beds in the waiting room.

The same life-and-death scenarios that are over-dramatized on TV were managed matter-of-factly, with an amp of epinephrine for a failing heart being ordered with the same emotion as the pancakes and sausages at 5:30 breakfast in the cafeteria. Making the trip back and forth from the call room to the ICU so frequently, and being so tired that late one night he had crawled into the portable laundry bin just outside the ICU and had buried himself in blankets and sheets until he was awakened by movement and rumbling. He had pulled back the blanket to the wide eyes and scream of the Hispanic housekeeper who had been pushing the bin down a ramp, but who had then let go, allowing the bin to speed up, career off a wall and dump him onto the tile floor amid a flurry of Spanish of which he only understood a reference to *"Madre Maria."*

He thought of Eddie, the surgery resident who hated being on call more than any other, when Eddie was on his cardiac surgery rotation and had a call room next to his. Eddie was getting paged or called every fifteen to twenty minutes all night every night; each beep or

215

ring was followed by a resonating "*goddammit*" until one night, at three in the morning, the curse was followed by a snap and a crash as the phone was ripped off the wall. The phone and pager went through the unopened window and into the courtyard seven floors below. Eddie went on to do a fellowship in plastic surgery and at last correspondence had a successful practice in cosmetics in LA.

His thoughts went back to his first week of residency. There, working with a world-renowned liver surgeon, he had gotten called to the ER to see a 52-year-old lady from out east who had a cancer diagnosed in the back part of her liver. She had been told at three cancer institutes that the tumor was not surgically removable and that liver transplants were not yet being done for malignancy. She and her husband had sold their car and borrowed against their home to buy a twenty-foot motor home. They collected her medical records and x-rays and blindly came west to the Mecca of Healing, where Dr. Payne was just beginning to learn the trade.

The couple had just walked into the ER on a Sunday afternoon and told the receptionist their story. If nothing could be done, they were just going to get back in the motor home and keep heading west on a national park tour they had dreamed of since before their youngest child had left for college a year prior.

Dr. Payne had gone over her records and admitted her to the hospital for further testing. His attending surgeon had seen her the following morning. Two days later she underwent a five-hour surgery to remove the cancer; four years later he was still getting Christmas cards from her. He thought of the night before she was discharged when, walking through the parking lot behind the hospital just before dark, he had come upon the motor home her husband had been staying in. A grill was set up outside on the asphalt and the husband was just throwing on a steak. He had offered, and Dr. Payne had accepted, a dinner invitation and a second steak was placed above the coals. After eating they had chatted in lawn chairs on a lovely summer night, cold beers in hand.

For the previous week, they had traveled together on the same bus. He would continue on with his other patients, but the lady from out east and her husband would be getting off that bus to reboard their motor home, deciding to keep going west on that national park tour after her discharge. They sent him postcards from Mesa Verde, Estes Park, the Grand Canyon, and the Tetons. When they got back home, they spent three months selling their house and getting things in order before heading north along the coast toward Nova Scotia without any particular itinerary. They just kept traveling, realizing there were no guarantees of time, stopping to work what they could find when they ran low on money. For the remainder of his residency they kept in touch with him, and he kept the postcards tacked to the wall in his call room, their freedom a stark contrast to his own situation, as the one hundred-plus hour work weeks rolled together.

He had been exposed to a lot that first year, occasionally jotting down his experiences with a few other patients like Jacob Schmidt in late September:

> "After splashing cold water on my face and toweling it
> off, I threw a white lab coat over my blue scrubs and made

my way to the surgical floor. A surgical intern, I had been up most of the night with a particularly sick patient and had hurriedly gone door-to-door scanning charts prior to morning rounds with the senior resident and Dr. Addington. Because most of the patients were sleeping, and because I had hoped for a short nap myself, I was just reviewing the charts at the door without going in.

As I perused Mr. Schmidt's chart he called me into his room. He was sitting on his bed in front of an east-facing window as the first rays of morning sent fingers of light probing about his hospital room. He had been admitted through our emergency department with an obstruction of his stomach that prevented him from eating, resulting in a significant loss of weight. This problem was usually due to scarring from a long-standing ulcer of his stomach or a tumor.

His work-up had included a CT scan that was suspicious for cancer, as were endoscopic biopsies.

Mr. Schmidt was 62 years old, and had recently retired from his job at a paper mill in Oshkosh, Wisconsin where he had worked for 36 years. He and his wife spoke of how they looked forward to spending their retirement at their cabin on a lake in northern Michigan. Dr. Addington was familiar with the area and they compared notes on local restaurants and hotspots for smallmouth bass.

It was explained to them that surgery was the best option to relieve the obstruction. If a cancer was confirmed most of the stomach would be removed, along with the lymph nodes draining the stomach, and part of his small intestine hooked up to the remaining stomach. They were told that the goal of the surgery would be curative, but that large stomach cancers were notorious for having already spread by the time symptoms develop. Surgery was scheduled for the next morning.

Mrs. Schmidt, their three kids and several grandchildren wished him love and luck as he was moved to the transport cart for the trip to the operating room. At surgery, the mass that had been seen on CT was confirmed to be an aggressive cancer with extension into the adjacent tissues, and multiple sites of spread within the abdomen not seen on the CT scan. The proposed operation had been abandoned and a bypass performed from the stomach above the obstruction to small intestine downstream from it.

After surgery, while Mr. Schmidt was waking up in the recovery room, I was with Dr. Addington as he spoke to the family. He told them he had tolerated the anesthetic without difficulty and was out of the operating room. He then told them what had been found and what had been done. The family was understandably distraught and immediately asked about other treatments, first asking about chemo and radiation and then about alternative or experimental treatments. Dr. Addington had told them the oncologist would be by in a couple days to discuss that *with them.*

"When will you tell him?" and "How long does he have?" were answered with "Dr. Payne will stop by later tonight to tell Jacob what I just told you. When I come by in the morning we can answer some of the questions you have."

When I stopped by to check on Mr. Schmidt that night, with the effects of the anesthetic mostly worn off, he wanted to know what we had found. His entire family was there. They had not told him what they had been told earlier and were working hard at a false sense of cheeriness. When I told him what Dr. Addington had earlier told the family, Mr. Schmidt closed his eyes and leaned his head back as a solitary tear slid down his cheek. The cheeriness quickly melted away to muffled sobs. He opened his eyes, took a deep breath and asked "well, what now?" I told him what the family had been told earlier about Dr. Addington answering questions in the morning and the Oncology service seeing him later in the week, but that right now the important thing was his recovery from surgery, which started with keeping him comfortable and working on his coughing and breathing.

When Dr. Addington came by in the morning the family was already there. He again reviewed what had been found at surgery and what had been done. Several questions were again asked about other treatment options, which he deferred to the oncologist.

"How much time do I have?" was met with a pause, followed by "most things in nature, including survival from a bad cancer, happen on a bell-shaped curve" with Dr. Addington drawing a flattened bell in the air with the index finger of his right hand. "The center, tallest part of the bell is where things happen most commonly. For your particular cancer, being metastatic and looking aggressive under the microscope, that center part of the bell is probably 6-8 months without any additional treatment. The left side of that curve are patients who, for whatever reason, don't do as well and the right side of the curve are patients who do better than the average. It's important to note that the tail on that right side seldom goes all the way down to zero so that, with or without additional treatment, there are patients still alive at 5 years, either from a dramatic response to treatment which has pushed that curve to the right or simply due to co-existing with the cancer for an extended period of time. I can't tell you right now where on that curve you will be, but I am telling you that this is serious enough that it would be a good time to make sure that you have things in order and make sure that you have a detailed living will."

Over the next few days, Mr. Schmidt had been very depressed with occasional bursts of anger, did not cooperate with the nurses, and ate very little when he was allowed to do so. He had met with the oncology team and a follow-up appointment with them set for three weeks after discharge, to allow time to recover from surgery before starting any additional treatment. He had asked the Oncologist specific questions about the benefits and side effects of chemo and was unsure whether he wanted to go ahead with it. A volunteer from Hospice had also stopped by to talk with him and give him contact information.

The only times when his mood changed was when talking about his cabin, talking about how the maples would soon be changing color and the cool, clear nights with the stars not competing with light from the city. Other than those moments Mr. Schmidt had remained sullen, refusing to get out of bed and eat or drink anything, so his IV needed to be restarted to keep him hydrated.

That morning I was surprised when he called me into his room and was sitting on the edge of his bed, facing the window, shaved and dressed.

"Morning," he said, "looks like you've up been all night again. Quite a sunrise out there, huh?"

Although glad he was feeling better, I was tired and in a hurry so I briefly glanced out the window and affirmed that it was a nice sunrise.

"When can I get out of here?" he asked.

"Looks like you're ready to go now. I'll be back to write your discharge orders and the nurses will have some paperwork, but you can probably get going by nine or so."

"Good", he said. "My son called last night from the cabin and said the maples are starting to turn. Figured that would be a good place to recover and sort things out. Might be my last fall up there."

I looked at him and then out the window, not in such a hurry anymore. The entire sky was afire with magenta, interspersed with soft linear clouds reflecting yellows and oranges.

"That is indeed quite a sunrise", I said with a smile, blinking a few times to clear the mist in my eyes as I turned toward the door.

Driving on, he recalled the increasing responsibility as his residency progressed. He remembered Edith Wilkins, an elderly local woman, who had come to the hospital with abdominal pain, fever, and low blood pressure. Upon getting her settled into the ICU the medicine team diagnosed her with an infected gallbladder and septic shock, given IV fluids and antibiotics and called for a surgery consult. Dr. Payne scrubbed out of an operation he was assisting with to evaluate her and after conferring with his attending surgeon, who was in the OR, made arrangements for Mrs. Wilkins to go to surgery. His attending was running two other operating rooms that day, and Dr. Payne had been told to go ahead and get started in a third. This was pre-laparoscopic cholecystectomy times, and the incision was an oblique one parallel to the lowest rib on the right. Using the intercom to inform his attending that the gallbladder was tensely swollen and gangrenous, he had been told to drain the gallbladder to decompress it, and start dissecting out the small bile tube connecting the gallbladder to the main bile duct.

Dr. Payne had assisted on dozens of gallbladder removals and had been guided through several, but none like this one. With difficulty he was able to doubly tie and divide both the bile duct and artery to the gallbladder; taking care to identify and avoid the larger common bile duct, the conduit for bile between the liver and duodenum. He then noticed his attending peering into the wound from behind the ether screen, standing next to the CRNA who was providing the anesthesia, fluids, meds, and plasma. The ether screen has been referred to as the "blood/brain barrier".

"That's a nasty one. I'll be next door if you need me."

The interface between the gallbladder and the liver had been very inflamed, and the liver bled profusely as the gangrenous gallbladder was finger-dissected and scooped away from it, made worse by a clotting deficiency from the severe infection. The attending called in to ask how it was going.

"Well, gallbladder's out, but she's still pretty wet; temp is down to ninety-four, her pressures are still low, and she hasn't made much urine since we started."

"Pack it for ten minutes by the clock. Then start closing. She'll clot better when she warms up."

Ten minutes later the bleeding had slowed considerably, and he had tried cauterizing and applying hemostatic gauze to a couple of spots that were still oozing, without much success. The anesthesiologist had given her plasma to help her blood clot and she had been started on a medication to raise her blood pressure over eighty, which also pushed her heart rate up over one-twenty.

Mrs. Wilkins had made very little urine since admission, and he remembered the nearly empty urine bag hanging at her bedside in the recovery room. That night she had a rocky course with dropping blood pressure, continued sluggish urine output and decreased oxygenation of her blood. He checked her hematocrit in the recovery room and twice in the intensive care unit. Each time it had dropped from previous, and he crossed matched her for two units of packed red blood cells and gave her additional plasma. Around ten o'clock he left the hospital, but was on the phone a couple of times an hour to the ICU, either answering nurses' questions or calling himself to see how she was doing. By three in the morning, he hadn't slept and figured he might as well head back to the hospital since he wasn't sleeping anyway. He figured they'd be taking her back to surgery later that night to stop the bleeding - if she didn't bleed to death first. He lived three blocks away and walked through downtown to get there. A misting rain had begun in the quiet late summer darkness. This was before the ubiquitous cell-phone and pages were answered from the corner pay phones he knew all too well.

Arriving at the hospital, he decided to hold off on going in and just walked around outside. The mist added a glow to the streetlights with a Londonesque effect. He found himself at an outdoor pool within an enclosed courtyard gazing at a life-sized bronze sculpture of "The Boy and the Dolphin." The sculpture glistened with pre-dawn moisture, the free-spirited youth holding onto the dorsal fin of the leaping dolphin with his left hand and the boy's other arm and legs flying away from his body.

He smiled, looked again at the boy, again at the dolphin, then got up and started back toward the hospital. The clouds seemed to be breaking up and the rain lightened with a few more people on the sidewalks in this 24/7 community of care. There had been no pages from the hospital since he arrived at that fountain. It was going to be OK.

The walk in the rain was *déjà vu* for another night, similarly spent, while working at the University Hospital in surgery and the ICUs as a monitor tech. He had gotten to know a 22-year-old woman with cystic fibrosis from her many previous admissions for respiratory distress. She had always come in with labored, rapid, wheezy breathing and within a few hours would be improved and would generally be discharged the following day. She was a year younger than he was, and had a passion for horses and riding. Working nights, there often wasn't a lot going on, so he would stop by her room to talk, and had gotten a birthday card from her, although he didn't remember telling her the date.

On this particular night she had again come in with respiratory distress which didn't seem much different from her previous episodes except that the doctors and nurses seemed more concerned, more of them were more involved and moving more quickly than on previous admissions. She had required intubation at least once before, so when they did an awake naso-trachial intubation, it hadn't triggered in him that this episode was any different. The look in Carrie's eyes, however, did tell him that this was different - they reflected a level of fear and panic that he hadn't seen in her before. His eyes had been the last eyes Carrie's eyes looked into before she arrested.

After forty-five minutes of chest compression, electric shocks, and protocols of medications the resuscitation had been stopped. He had stood there in disbelief as the monitors were turned off; no tears, no feeling at all, numbness. He had just left his equipment at the bedside and walked out of the ICU, out of the hospital into a night very much like this night – calm and warm with a misting drizzle that slowly soaked the scrubs he was wearing. He had walked away from the hospital, ignoring the pages coming from the bulky, noisy, low-tech pager at his waist. An hour or so later, at four in the morning, he wound up back at the hospital, back at the department office. In fewer than five minutes, he had written the essay portion to his medical school application, an essay which the assistant dean later told him had caught the attention of the admission's committee more than his less than stellar undergraduate performance.

Thoughts of Carrie faded as the past gave way to the present, to Mrs. Wilkins. Soon it was five o'clock and the earliest of morning traffic started as the city began to waken. Making another pay phone call to the ICU he realized that this was just nuts, that he couldn't spend the rest of his life like this, walking around outside the hospital all night waiting for his patients to crash. Maybe he had gotten into more than he could handle.

At 6:30 rounds with the attending Mrs. Wilkins looked surprisingly good with improvements in her vital signs and urine output. After examining her and looking over the nurses' charting, the labs and orders, the attending had left a brief note and commented, "looks like a routine gallbladder."

Dr. Payne had started to disagree, but then realized that the attending knew the night he had had, knew how the feeling of responsibility had hit him square in the face, knew there was nothing routine about it from his standpoint. The attending knew that because he had been there himself.

Morning rounds had gone well. He had a few minutes to go back to his call room to clean up a bit before heading down to the operating room. While shaving he noticed a quote on his wall from a surgical pioneer he had been privileged to train with at the University who, recalling his own days as a surgical resident had written:

> *"Reaching far back, I remember in my junior resident days, after working all night, having a few moments to catch the sunrise before a quick breakfast, morning rounds and going to the operation room, I recall that in those moments I had the sensation that life does not get any better."*

It was now nearly a decade later, and Dr. Payne still had nights like that, sleepless nights, worrying about the latest Mrs. Wilkins. The difference was now those patients were members of the community he lived in rather than the wide-ranging patient base inherent to a major medical center. Those sleepless nights and distracted days took a toll. The rewards were many, but the occasions when things didn't go well were tough.

He remembered a few of the nine patients that walked out of the hospital after emergent surgery for a ruptured abdominal aortic aneurysm, remembering all four that didn't. He had operated on all thirteen with the same scrub nurse. Whether or not she was on call, Virginia was always available for the big cases. They had worked together during his residency and found themselves at the same community hospital. Dr. Payne seldom had to ask for a specific instrument because Virginia was always a step ahead of him, and would have it ready before he extended his hand in her direction, surgical choreography at its best.

He thought of how different his life would have been if he had actually gotten a job in wildlife biology after college, or if the Peace Corps assignment to South Yemen hadn't been canceled two weeks before his departure because a civil war with North Yemen had broken out; or if he hadn't been fired from his bartending job at the Holiday Inn Viking Lounge, just as he was being considered for a promotion to bar manager, because he had given out too many free drinks to old high school friends. He wound up working in surgery at the University Hospital, which rekindled an old flame first ignited while working in sterile supply, cleaning bed pans in the basement of the same eleven hundred bed hospital where he had later done his surgical residency. It was there that he would sneak up to the old-time operating theater and watch surgery from the tiled bleachers, watching the masters in action. He was not as impressed with the surgeons themselves as he was with the trust the patients put in those surgeons; the patients allowing themselves to be put asleep and opened up with broken or diseased parts being removed, repaired, or replaced. The flame was again rekindled during an interim study between undergrad semesters spent working in a cardiovascular research dog lab of that same institution testing heart valves and pacemakers.

The previous day he had removed the upper lobe of the left lung of a 62-year-old man who had been smoking since he was 14, the lobe containing a golf-ball-sized cancer. As usual, he had paused during the operation to marvel at the beautiful anatomy within the chest. He looked beyond the normally pink, now gray, bi-lobed lung, filled with millions of tiny gas exchange sacs, which in this fellow had coalesced into far fewer sacs far less efficient in gas exchange. He located the nerves to the diaphragm and stomach as they passed near the translucent sac around the heart, within which the heart was beating away, as it had since ten days after conception, despite not having been particularly well cared for. He also marveled at the finger-sized pulmonary vessels which carried spent blood to the lungs for reoxygenation, and then back to the four-chambered muscle that technology had been unable to replicate, from which it would forcefully be pumped out to the rest of the body.

He recalled the med-school project where fetal rat hearts had been removed and diced, the connective tissues dissolved away with an enzyme. The heart cells were then plated out on a culture medium, and observed under a microscope. He hadn't known what to expect, but had become discouraged as the culture appeared to be overgrown with unwanted endothelial cells. On the ninth day, expecting the worst as he peered into the microscope under high power, the entire culture was beating at a ventricular rate of forty beats per minute; electrical, chemical, invisible connections having been restored between the cells. Two days later the culture was completely overgrown, and the beating stopped.

There was no direct clinical application for the project, but the moment he first saw the culture beating had stayed with him, as had the first heart transplant he assisted with as a resident, when the donor heart was sewed into the recipient, warmed and lightly shocked with electrical paddles. The transplanted heart hesitated for just a moment before starting to beat, weakly at first and then with enough force to do what it had to do to make that man well again. He had also been part of the surgical team that had gone by jet to Kansas City to harvest that donor heart. He remembered it was a Monday night, because the Chiefs were playing under the lights at Arrowhead Stadium as they flew by on their way to the airport, where a van was waiting for them on the tarmac, along with a police escort to Truman County Hospital. It had been his first time on a private jet, and he remembered being excited by the amenities, leg room and unlimited snacks; excited, that is, until the attending surgeon came by with a twenty-eight-page harvest protocol for him to review before they landed forty-five minutes later.

He remembered the scrub room with a large glass window looking into the over-sized operating room, through which they could see the white-coated residents and med students lining up on bleachers against the far wall, then backing through the swinging door after a ten minute scrub, hands away from his body at eye level, water dripping from his elbows, a surprisingly festive mood in the OR with the Beatles "Get Back" playing as they started slipping into gowns and gloves. Years before that in undergrad, he had a pet crow, coincidentally named JoJo. Years after that, throughout his career, patients of his named Loretta would bring him back to that moment.

He remembered that it had been his responsibility to carry the heart back home in a Playmate cooler, the heart having been flushed with a preservative solution similar to ones he had helped research in med school, where they had studied the role of ribose in the ATP metabolic pathway. He remembered that the donor heart had been from a black man and the recipient had been white, surprising to him that they had successfully cross-matched. He remembered that a lot of things surprised him back in those days, realized that a lot still did.

He thought of how different his life might have been if, in June of 1968, at ten years old, he had not heard Ted Kennedy's eulogy of his brother Bobby as being "a good and decent man, who saw wrong and tried to right it, saw suffering and tried to heal it, saw war and tried to stop it." Those haunting words had subconsciously guided his intentions, if not always his actions. He thought of his own eulogy - and *where he saw pus, he tried to drain it.* All this and more passed through his head as he drove to the hospital, sliding through red lights because no one else was on the road.

It was nights like this that Dr. Steven Payne thought of his plan for retirement, a side-by-side tackle shop and outpatient surgery clinic in northern Minnesota, all cash, that he would call Bait n' Stitch. He knew he'd have issues with the Department of Health but figured he could work that out.

Chapter Twenty-Four

Without much chitchat, Dr. Payne had explained what he was going to do as he put in the scope and filled the man's rectum with air, allowing good visualization of the plastic tube. He then lassoed it with the snare before pulling on the wire with his right hand and guiding the tube out of the rectum with the index finger of his left. A quick dictation, a note on the ER record, and he was off to start morning hospital rounds before his first scheduled surgery at 7:30.

The hazelnut flavored coffee he had grabbed at the hospital cafeteria had not yet fully cut through the fog of the sleep-deprived by the time he saw his next-to-last patient, Mary Keilen, a 64-year-old woman who had undergone a left mastectomy for an aggressive breast cancer involving multiple arm pit lymph nodes two days prior. Mary had been very calm and matter-of-fact about her diagnosis, the loss of a breast and the pending chemotherapy. This morning, as Dr.

Payne looked her over and discussed discharge instructions, with a follow-up appointment to have her drains taken out and to see the oncologist, she was more anxious and tearful than she had been. He assumed that she had finally realized the seriousness of her situation. When she told him that she hadn't slept well the night before, he asked her if she was worried about either her prognosis or the toxic effects of the upcoming chemo. She told him no, all of that was out of her hands so there was no reason to worry about it. What had kept her awake was wondering if she would be able to make it, that day, to the first family visitation at the Hazelden Treatment Center, where her son had been taken two weeks prior for a heroin addiction that had nearly destroyed his life - and the lives of those around him. With adrenal glands and the caffeine finally kicking in, he was more labile than he realized, and Mary's only concern being for her son in the midst of her own tragedy pushed him over. His voice broke, badly, as he tried to say the right thing. Yes, she could certainly go to visit her son he informed her, after recomposing himself.

"It'll be okay," she reassured him, putting his hands in her own.

"That was supposed to be my line," he said, their eyes connecting, saying more than words had. As he descended the back stair from the Women's Center to the med-surg floor to see the new consult, he thought of the quiet dramas being played out in the daily lives of ordinary people. Mary was still on his mind as he walked into Frank's room after reviewing the chart at his door.

Dr. Payne introduced himself to Frank and Jimmy. After getting a brief medical history from Frank and examining him, he sat on the edge of the bed. Speaking deliberately and focusing his attention primarily on Frank, he asked him if he'd heard the results of the scan. Frank responded that he hadn't.

"The scan was done to look for possible spread of the cancer that Dr. Pizini found in your colon yesterday," Dr. Payne began. "There appears to be tumor in both sides of your liver, which is most likely spread from the colon cancer. Prostate cancer more commonly goes to bone, which yours already has. The oncologist may recommend a needle biopsy of the tumor in your liver to confirm that."

Dr. Payne paused to gauge Frank's reaction before continuing.

"Doesn't sound good," was Frank's only response.

"The portion of colon where your cancer started is relatively easy to remove and you wouldn't need a bag afterward. Even though the cancer is large, it doesn't appear to be causing a blockage, but it may continue to slowly bleed. There would be some increased risk with surgery because of the stroke you had. The tumor in your liver will be difficult to treat. We're probably looking at months instead of years, and the surgery would set you back for at least some of your remaining time. I just don't think it would help you much in the long run. Your blood count can be followed and you can get another transfusion if it gets too low again.

'Frank, you've had a tough year with the stroke, the recurrent prostate cancer, and now this. You have several horses dragging you toward a cliff and we just don't have the bullets to stop them all."

A nurse entered Frank's room "Dr. Payne, the OR is calling. You need to go down and sign the consent for your first surgical patient."

"Tell them I'll be right down."

Turning back to Frank, Dr. Payne continued, "Dr. Kumani is the oncologist who will be coming by to talk to you about other treatment options. She's really smart, and I think you'll like her. I'll stop back myself between surgeries to see if there are any questions I can answer."

As Dr. Payne started toward the door, there was an overhead page for him to call down to the OR.

On the way to the operating room, Dr. Payne thought of rose gardens he had been taken to on a grade school field trip to a local doctor's country home. He remembered the gardens themselves with a variety of colors, especially the sea of red ones. He remembered spending most of the time trying to catch one of the foot-long goldfish in a sculpted pond closer to the house until he was reprimanded and taken back to the bus. He had assumed that the doctor was retired and had nothing better to do than grow flowers. He later found out that the doctor was an oncologist in his forties at the time, still practicing at the same medical center where he was learning to be a surgeon. That oncologist still had the rose gardens - gardens he had started as an escape from his days spent with cancer patients. The roses were an escape from patients living scan to scan, lab test to lab test, biopsy to biopsy, the celebrated successes and the all too common failures, the difficult discussions. The gardens were an escape from too many patients made sicker by treatments that had little effect on their malignancies, with too much of their remaining "good time" spent shuffling back and forth to appointments, testing and procedures; too much of this time spent worrying and puking. In his garden a more predictable, a more positive result from his work was assured. He could plant, water, and fertilize, pull the weeds himself and bask in the same sun his roses were basking in.

When he thought of "good time" in a medical context, Dr. Payne thought of how relative that could be. He thought of Roger, the 55-year-old member of his church with severe multiple sclerosis, wheelchair parked in the aisle every Sunday, his wife in the pew next to him, able to communicate only with his keypad, always flashing a crooked but genuine smile at any interaction. He had very little interaction with Roger until he came to the emergency department by ambulance throwing up blood. Dr. Payne had seen Roger shortly after arrival. His heart rate was in the mid-100s and his blood pressure in the 70s, IV fluids wide open, O negative blood on the way.

Roger was still alert enough to participate in the discussion Dr. Payne had with him and his wife. Considering the severity of his neuromuscular status, the first decision was whether to do anything about the bleeding which was likely due to an ulcer that had eroded into an artery. Endoscopy would be the initial intervention with an attempt to stop the bleeding with heater probe cauterization, injection of epinephrine to constrict the bleeding vessel or placement of small metal clips. Dr. Payne's hospital did not have the capability of trying to stop the bleeding with angiography and embolization. If the bleeding could not be stopped with endoscopy, then surgery would be the next step.

With the first unit of blood hanging and with a blood pressure now in the 60s, Roger had used the keypad to say "yes" to both questions. Dr. Payne then asked Roger if he wanted to be resuscitated if his heart should stop beating. Again, using the keyboard he pounded out "yes", and then "I still have a lot to live for".

At endoscopy, the stomach was full of fresh blood which was evacuated well enough to see that the brisk bleeding was coming from an ulcer in the first portion of the duodenum just past the stomach - bleeding that could not be controlled through the scope. An operating room was already set up and waiting when the decision was made to proceed to surgery.

Roger coded and was intubated on his way to the OR, chest compressions being done as his abdomen was prepped and draped. An upper abdominal incision was made, the duodenum opened and suctioned of blood, the bleeding ulcer identified, oversewn with deep sutures and the artery feeding the ulcer tied off. A heart rhythm and blood pressure returned.

Roger was wheeled out of the hospital five days later, and was back in church two weeks after that. Dr. Payne hadn't really thought much about Roger until the Sunday morning when he wasn't in his usual spot, his wife still in hers. After the service Dr. Payne had talked with her in the narthex. She said that Roger had died peacefully at home, and she thanked Dr. Payne for giving Roger three more good years. The word "good" had stuck with him, such a relative term.

Chapter Twenty-Five

D r. Payne had finished his afternoon surgery with repair of a belly button hernia on a patient who had been having symptoms of intermittent bowel obstruction over the previous month or so. He had seen Olav Torseth the day before in surgery clinic when, after reviewing his chart and medical history, Dr. Payne had seen what he had expected as he walked into the exam room; a haggard, seemingly gaunt elderly fellow showing signs of alcoholic cirrhosis. He noted that three days prior Olav had six liters of fluid drained from his distended abdomen to lessen his discomfort, fluid resulting from his sick liver. Clinic had been running late and Dr. Payne anticipated a relatively brief appointment to evaluate the hernia and make sure that he was medically fit for even a minor surgery. The primary concern with the repair itself would be to ensure that it was water-tight so there would be no leakage of reaccumulating fluid through the repair.

Despite the weathered appearance Mr. Torseth had an alert twinkle in his eyes and a relaxed smile on his lips. After examining Olav and reviewing his medical history, after talking about the surgery itself and what to expect, and after deciding to proceed the following day, they somehow got talking about how Olav had been a commercial fisherman on Lake Superior. This had been before and during the decimation of the lake trout population caused by the combination of overfishing and the infestation of sea lampreys, which had come through the St. Lawrence Seaway from the Atlantic Ocean decades prior. Olav said they initially had started noticing just the scars on the trout they caught; later seeing the actual lampreys themselves, eel-like parasitic creatures, often greater than a foot in length, hanging off the fish, attached by their horny teeth and suction mouth, the razor-like tongue having penetrated the fish's scales so they could suck the life blood out of their prey. Soon they started also seeing lampreys and scars on the kamloops and larger herring. Their catches continued to decline until they were out of the commercial fishing business.

"Many salmon back in those days?

"Yeah, there were silvers and some of the kings got up to thirty pounds, but we lived and died with the lakers."

Olav had grown up and fished out of Knife River, a small town near Two Harbors, on the Minnesota north shore. Dr. Payne was familiar with the town because he had fished for steelhead on the Knife River and several of the other streams between there and the Canadian border. They traded smelting stories, which led into Dr. Payne asking Olav about the drinking. Olav said he had mostly drank Black Velvet whiskey and "a little Christian Brothers brandy." After the collapse of the fishing industry, he spent most of his days making cabinets in a woodworking shop attached to his house on a wooded lot near the lake. Living alone, he had switched to cheap vodka, mixing it "about half and half" with water in a never-empty coffee cup. Olav had started noticing the yellowing of his eyes. His skin had become itchy, and his belly swollen. Following a reluctant visit to a local nurse practitioner and a battery of tests, she had called him at home with the results. At ten in the morning, in his shop, vodka-water in one hand and phone in the other, he had been told that he had near end-stage cirrhosis of his liver and would die in the ensuing weeks if he kept drinking. Olav had hung up the phone, emptied the remaining poison in his cup out the open window and hadn't had a drink since then.

"You quit just like that?" Dr. Payne asked with a note of skepticism.

"Sure did. I believed her when she told me I was killing myself and I wasn't ready to be done."

It was now seven years later. He made it back to the North Shore fishing, not in the lake itself but in the streams that fed that lake, and not with nets but with a fly-rod, not for lake trout but for brookies. His liver was still bad, but his eyes were no longer yellow, and his life was good.

Shortly before seeing Olav to have him sign the consent for surgery, the admitting nurse had called Dr. Payne to tell him there was a problem: Mr. Torseth had been drinking. His heart sunk, as he had become as attached to this fellow as much as a person can in a twenty minute office visit.

"How much did he drink?'

"Just one cup of coffee in the waiting area, but anesthesia says he can't have any sedation for another two hours."

"Coffee? No alcohol?"

Audibly sighing after confirmation, "that shouldn't be a problem." Olav had been given the option of waiting a couple hours so he could have intravenous sedation along with the local anesthesia or just going with straight local, which could be done without delay. He chose the latter and went home shortly after the procedure was completed.

By the time Dr. Payne stopped by Frank's room, Frank and Jimmy had already talked it over with Dr. Kumani, had met with the hospice team, and Frank had been discharged.

Two weeks later, Kelly came through the screen door into the kitchen, after working the night shift, as Jimmy was putting away his breakfast dishes.

"I can't believe they named an airport after that asshole!" she said, tossing the truck keys onto the counter.

"What asshole?"

"Dulles, that creep that used the CIA to overthrow the government of Guatemala so United Fruit could keep their little banana republic. Led to the civil war that set 'em back forty years, made 'em the poorest country in Latin America."

"What brought on that little outburst?" Jimmy asked, somewhat amused.

"I finally got around to reading that book, <u>Bitter Fruit,</u> I got when I spent two weeks at the Catholic mission in San Lucas Toliman on Lake Atitlan in Guatemala, working with Father Gregg on a reforesting project. I just feel so bad for what we did to them. The government was trying to put in some of the same reforms that FDR was doing here. Dulles labeled them communists to justify it."

"Yeah, he and his brother should have gone to prison as war criminals. They were responsible for a similar coup in Iran that contributed to the Islamic Revolution and the rise of the fundamentalism we are dealing with now."

"How do you know that?"

"I don't remember a lot from high school, but that one stuck with me."

"By the way, I had the lump taken out yesterday."

"What lump?"

"The breast lump," Kelly replied, pointing to her right chest.

"You did? When did you decide to do that?"

"It seemed a little bigger and more tender, so I called the surgeon. Did it under local anesthesia with IV sedation at the outpatient surgery center. Jenny gave me a ride home afterward."

"Why didn't you tell me? Is it okay?"

"Yeah, the pathologist looked at it after it came out. Says it's benign, a fibroadenoma like they thought it was on the needle biopsy. I am glad to have it out of there and know it's nothing to worry about."

"So am I. Did it hurt?"

"No, I was pretty out of it for the procedure and didn't remember much. No stitches or anything that have to come out. It's all absorbable suture under the skin with a little butterfly tape over the top. Just kind of sore."

"Where are Frank and Alice?"

"That Herman guy who had the New Year's Eve party rented a limo to take a bunch of old folks up to Turtle Lake Casino. Frank was pretty fired up. I think they were both ready for a road trip. He said it might be late when they got back and told me we didn't have to wait up. The transfusion he got a couple weeks ago did seem to perk him up although I'm not sure how long it will last. He told me last night that he's done with doctors, hospitals, having his blood drawn, the whole thing. He likes having the hospice folks come out, but decided to stop all his medications except the stuff for pain and to just let nature take its course."

"Can't say I disagree with him after all he's been through."

"Looks like we have the day to ourselves. It's gorgeous outside. I was gonna do some yard work while you sleep. I thought we could go biking later and then have a bonfire and picnic down by the pond tonight. I could show you how I was thinking the house could be laid out."

"Perfect. Wake me up at two if I'm still sleeping."

The weather held and the evening at the pond went as planned. Kelly was just leaving for work when the limo pulled up. She and Jimmy helped Frank and Alice out and back into their wheelchairs, chatted with Herman and Helga for a few moments, and started back up the ramp to the house. Frank didn't have the energy he thought he would have, and had spent most of the afternoon sleeping in the limo while the others gambled, most playing the machines, with Herman spending the day at a two-dollar blackjack table. Alice held up better than Frank, but did join him for a couple-hour nap in the late afternoon. She enjoyed the excitement of the rows of clanging machines, and had one of the aides that Herman hired do the mechanics for her - putting the coins into the slot and pulling the levers.

Alice had started the day with $100 in quarters and had just enough left by dinnertime to go to the all-you-can-eat seafood buffet. Helga had been the big winner, hitting a $1,200 jackpot on Joker Poker with others hitting a few smaller jackpots on the quarter slots.

The road trip had gone well, but it would be Frank's last time off the farm.

Less than a month later, Frank was surprisingly alert for having a blood pressure below seventy systolic. He hadn't been out of bed for the previous ten days, and wasn't eating or drinking much. With the dehydration, his pain became much easier to control and he no longer needed the morphine suppositories and suspensions to augment the fentanyl patch that was changed every third day.

It was evening and Jack was sitting in Frank's room on a folding chair by his bed. "Jack, tell me about your first train trip."

"Well, we started off at that Northtown yard up in Fridley. Didn't have a computerized schedule so we just went out to the train yard around midnight, found a switchman and asked him to show us a train heading west. We thought he'd kick us out of the yard, which is probably what he'd do now, but then he not only took us to the train, but found us a cushioned car. Said it would get going around four in the morning, which it did.

'We took along some big wood screws and screwed them into the three-quarter-inch plywood lining the cars and hung hammocks to sleep in. Went past the St. Cloud prison and then parallel to Interstate 94 for quite a while, going about the same speed as the traffic. The train stopped in Dilworth, which is just this side of Moorhead, and then took off again. I remember just before sunset going through the wetlands out by Jamestown, North Dakota, with the ducks setting their wings over a sea of goldenrod before dropping into the potholes. I know what you meant when you said the evenings on the train were the best, wondering where you'd be come morning.

'We stopped once during the night, just this side of Minot at the Gavin Yards, and then went past the east entrance of Glacier Park shortly after the sun came up. Man, was it cold, even snowed for a while and this was in June. We crossed a river gorge in Idaho on a bridge that must have been five hundred feet above the water.

'Funny, the things you remember. As we crossed the bridge we were sitting in the open doorway eating Spam and mustard sandwiches. The cold Spam put a lardy glaze over the roof of my mouth that was tough to get rid of. That night we stopped in Spokane, Washington, just as it was getting dark. It was the only place we really saw many hobos. There were dozens of campfires on the edge of the train yard and there was a liquor store about a hundred yards from the tracks, so my buddy ran over and bought a six-pack of beer. The train was just getting going as he hopped back on.

'That night we went through a couple long tunnels in the Cascades; the diesel about suffocated us. At around seven in the morning, we got to the coast at Everett. Followed the Sound down to Seattle and at ten in the morning we hopped off a couple hundred yards from the King Dome. We tried to check into a dumpy hotel to clean up and get some sleep, but the guy at the desk said we were too filthy, so we headed down to the wharf to check it out. We didn't have any real plans other than to hang around Seattle a couple of days and then hop a train back to Minnesota, but somehow we figured out we had enough money for a single one-way ticket on the MV Columbia to Alaska - a hundred fifty bucks or so.

'Anyway, the ferry was just getting ready to leave so we bought a ticket. I went aboard, wrapped up the stub in some aluminum foil and tossed it off the upper deck to my buddy who was on the dock. He made up some story about how he had to go back to his car for something, like we even had a car within two thousand miles. So, next thing we know, we're on a three-day trip up the Inland Passage to Alaska, sleeping out on the deck with fifty or sixty other kids who couldn't afford the cabins.

'We stopped in Peterson, Ketchikan, and then Juneau, where half the boat got off at two in the morning and went to the Red Dog Saloon. Got to Haines, Alaska, with seventeen dollars between the two of us and hitchhiked from there. A guy picked us up in Tok, Alaska. He had been an architect in LA and got stuck in the same traffic he had gotten stuck in every other day. He decided he'd had enough and just kept heading north. He had an orange VW with bad brakes. We went down a big hill by the Matanuska Glacier and he was pumping the parking brake to slow us down. We rode with him to Anchorage; he paid for a motel room for the three of us for a few days. I think he called his roommate back in LA to have some of his stuff put into storage and the rest sent to Anchorage.

'We bummed around the Kenai Peninsula for a while and went up to McKinley and Fairbanks. We passed up a ride with a geologist to Prudhoe Bay, which I wish we would have taken. We did a few odd jobs here and there, like mopping floors in a fish cannery in Seward, but we were broke and hungry most of the summer. We'd just stand outside restaurants watching people eat through the window. We did a lot of dumpster diving. It's surprising how much good food gets thrown away. We decided our life goal was to someday be so well off financially that we could go to McDonald's anytime we wanted and order anything we wanted. It actually seemed unrealistic at the time. The greatest part of the trip was that we had everything we needed on our backs and had total freedom."

Following a thoughtful pause, Frank said softly, "Imagine I'll be traveling pretty light from here on out myself. Did you know Jimmy took his truck up to Alaska?"

"Yeah, we compared notes," Jack replied.

"So you didn't tell me how you got back."

"We hitchhiked back on the Al-Can Highway that Jimmy was on, some of it in a van with a half dozen other kids, mostly from Europe. I would like to go back up some day and get out to some of the more remote areas. There wasn't much of the state we could get to by road."

"Jack, this past year out of boredom, I've watched more damn television than I had in my whole life before that. A lot of it was garbage, but there were some good shows about places that I would have liked to have seen, beautiful places." Coughing, but gathering steam as Jimmy walked in, Frank continued "some of the places were man-made, but the best were the untouched natural places, vast and wonderful places, from the rain forests to the Himalayas, to the Serengeti, to the Arctic, to the bottom of the ocean. I especially liked the shows about the magnificent migrations - birds from warblers to whooping cranes, caribou and wildebeest, monarch butterflies, salmon. We take bees for granted, but they may be the most incredible creatures of them all.

'Most of my life was spent outdoors trying to make a living off the soil, living season to season, feeling a part of the land I farmed. Some of the things I saw on TV make me worried about what my generation has done to the world that we are passing on to your generation. Saw a special on polar bears in northern Norway, way the hell up in the Arctic, remotest damn place you can imagine. Anyway, scientists found near toxic levels of PCB's in 'em, figured the air currents from Europe carried them to the Arctic and they came down with the rain and snow. Since the bears are at the top of the food chain, they're screwed. Hate to think of all the stuff we're exposed to; maybe that's how I got one or both of my cancers.

'You watch the news every night and hear about disappearing rain forests, melting glaciers, once majestic rivers being turned into open sewers. You can't eat the fish out of what used to be pristine lakes and streams. Entire species are disappearing right and left including indicator species like frogs. Seal pups are drowning at birth because their mothers can't find ice to give birth on. It seems like the canaries are dying in their cages all around us. We can't keep letting our moment in the sun spoil it for those who follow us."

Looking at Jimmy, Frank then pointed to the nightstand that had a white envelope and a small wooden box on top. "Open the envelope."

A bit puzzled, Jimmy did as he was told. Looking inside he scanned its contents, "Wow, Frank! Plane tickets and reservations for Jack and me tarpon fishing in Costa Rica."

Jack, jumping in, "Jimmy, wait till you see the tape. You won't believe the fishing we're gonna have."

"Oh, I've seen the tape and was actually looking forward to going with Frank someday."

Frank smiled, "That makes two of us, Jimmy."

Jack, more subdued, "Frank, it really won't be the same without you."

"Bullshit. Open the box."

Jack flipped the latch and opened what turned out to be a humidor with two thick, nearly black, Dominican cigars. "At the end of your perfect day, when you're standing around the fire on the beach telling stories, light those mothers up and I'll be there."

"Frank, when did you do all of this?" Jack asked.

"After the bone scan, I figured it was gonna be kind of rough going, so I started getting a few things in order."

"Frank, you're the best," Jimmy started. "I talked to Kelly about naming our first boy Frank, but she really didn't like the name, not even as a middle name. So instead, after I sell the Holsteins, I'm gonna get a half dozen Angus cows and a big ass bull. I'm gonna name him Frank and when we haul his shaggy ass to the butcher we'll name the next one Frank, Jr."

"Touching."

Jack opened his mouth to start a similar course of drivel, but Frank cut him off. Barely audible, "Jimmy, look under the cigars. There is a quote out of one of your books that I found last week. Can you read it and then help Alice back in?"

Jimmy began, after lifting the recipe card from the box, "Looks like Thoreau," Jimmy noted as he scanned the passage before beginning:

> *"We had a remarkable sunset one day last November. I was walking in a meadow, the source of a small brook, when the sun at last, just before setting, after a cold, gray day, reached a clear stratum in the horizon... It was such a light as we could not have imagined a moment before, and the air was so warm and serene that nothing was wanting to make a paradise of that meadow."*

With Jimmy on her right and Jack on her left, Alice came into the room looking no better than Frank. The boys helped her into a stuffed chair next to the bed and closed the door quietly. The overhead light went off as Jack and Jimmy left, with the only remaining light coming from a ten-gallon aquarium on the dresser in which three unnamed goldfish swam with their noses to the glass, waiting to be fed.

Alice and Frank looked into each other's lifeless eyes, saying nothing as there was little left to say. Alice brushed back Frank's hair with the crooked fingers of her right hand and pushed back the covers with her left. Crawling into bed next to Frank, she kissed him on the cheek and laid her head on the pillow facing his.

"Are you comfortable?"

Frank nodded slowly with eyes closed.

"Are you afraid?"

Frank opened his eyes and brought his gaze up to hers. "This afternoon," he began haltingly with a gurgling deep in his chest and a cough he couldn't clear, "I must have been sleeping, but in the darkness, I could see a light in the distance. Coming from the light a man was walking toward me. I couldn't see his face because of the shadows, but I think it was Pa. He was reaching to me, and I was trying hard to see his face, but before I did, I woke up and couldn't get back to sleep.

"Alice, I'm tired, my time has come and I'm ready to go, but I really think we're going to see each other again."

Alice was momentarily buoyed at the thought of being with Frank again, both free of their current disabilities. William slipped back into her thoughts. He had died so suddenly they had hardly spoken before his death. She smiled to herself at the thought of introducing William to Frank and being introduced to Betty, and wondered how that whole thing would work out.

Her thoughts came back to the present and, although Frank's words embodied the cornerstone of her active faith, she couldn't suppress a level of doubt that she would really see Frank, or William, again.

During the night, as she felt the warmth leave Frank's body, a chill went through her own. Far away a train whistle blew. For Frank's sake, Alice wondered where it would be come morning. For herself she wondered what she would do without him. Alice could feel the bitterness that Frank had erased beginning its return as she was again left alone with her pain and frailty. This time she had wanted to go first.

———————

In the months that followed Frank's passing, Alice stayed at the farm, where she ate little and spoke little. Her two daughters had gone with her to Frank's funeral, and each spent a day a week taking her out for lunch and helping Kelly with wedding plans and farmhouse projects.

Frank had paid off the balance on the tennis bracelet, and Alice gave it to Kelly as an early wedding present. She got progressively weaker, and a couple of months after Frank's death, and a couple weeks before the wedding, Alice also died, in her sleep - alone but for the goldfish.

About the Author

Born and raised in Rochester, Minnesota, Kevin Bjork spent his summers playing baseball and exploring the Zumbro River with his mixed breed spaniel. He met his wife Evelyn at Gustavus Adolphus College in St. Peter, Minnesota where he was a wildlife biology major. Two years later, he began medical school at the University of Minnesota, followed by a residency in general surgery at the Mayo Clinic.

He and Evelyn settled in Stillwater, Minnesota, where they raised their four boys, and where he has been practicing general surgery since 1990. A past president of the Minnesota Surgical Society and co-founder of the Metro Mercenaries Rugby Football Club and the Moosehead Wide Open Charity Golf Tournament, Kevin is currently serving on the board of Hospitalito Atitlan in Santiago de Atitlan in Guatemala where he has led surgical mission trips for over twenty years.

Made in the USA
Monee, IL
18 July 2023